Daughter of Mine

Innocence Broken

T. West- Fields

ISBN: 9798537583394

DEDICATION

Dedicated to Constance (Connie) Harris, the best storyteller.

CONTENTS

ACKNOWLEDGMENTS

Jasmine Scott- Author
Aaron Harris- Photographer
Zaykia Drake- Model

CHAPTER ONE

Sasha is sitting at a grave site putting fresh flowers around the head stone crying profusely wondering, why is this happening to me. She says out loud, "My life is over." She began to think back to where it all went wrong, from what she can remember. It was a nice hot sunny day the afternoon they moved to Boynton Beach Florida. James Kingsley is a construction worker. When construction slows down, he does seasonal work in agriculture wherever it is available. He'd just moved the family from New York where they were picking cherries and apples. They took the children with them to work in the cherry fields, but they ate more than what they put in the bins. Barbara would work odd jobs depending on the area they moved to. For the most part she was either cooking or cleaning. Their children are young; Shannon is ten with an imagination out of this world. Most of the time is imagining she's living with another family. James Jr. is eight; he makes fun of everything and everybody so no one would notice his problems. The baby girl Sasha is six with a mind of a teenager. She is like an adventure waiting to happen, very curious and full of life. She keeps a positive outlook on life even when faced with conflict. Whatever Shannon learns she teach it to Sasha. The children were glad to be in Florida, they did not like New York at all. It was rough for Shannon who was always fighting off gangs to protect herself and her two siblings. Every time they move Shannon gets bullied because she is the new kid in the neighborhood. She hopes the kids here are not as bad as they were in New York. She is tired of being pushed around at school and at home. It took a week to get unpacked and two more to get settled in once again. James and Barbara got the children up early on Saturday morning and walked them two streets over to meet his brother and family. James never talked about nor visited his family much. The last time he went home to visit his dad they got into a fight, he hadn't been back to visit his dad since. The children only knew their mom's relatives; they were surprised and thrilled to meet their Uncle Robert and Aunt Pricilla. They had four children all younger than Sasha, three girls and one boy who was of course named Jr. Shannon was happy because it meant she had family to visit to get away from home. Toys were pulled out for the kids to play while the adults went outside to talk. Well the ladies talked; the men argued. Robert looking at James shaking his head side to side said, "James man you can't just pop up and visit acting like everything is normal and cheery. Why won't you let mom and dad know you're okay? You're acting stupid as hell not talking to your own parents." "Look Robert, I visit whoever the hell I want; you should be glad I visit you. Dammit man, get off my case. I don't visit mom because I have nothing to say to the old man and you know that." Robert wanted to hit James but decided not to. He had not seen his brother in twelve years. He got a letter from him every now and then. Besides, James was taller and stronger; it would be like trying to bring a mule down to his knees. Robert smiled to break the tension between them. He walked up to James and hugged him instead. "Good to see ya bro, what brings you down here?" James smiles at his brother to say, "Besides you man I got a job building houses this time. I hope it last my kids getting tired of moving. I want to try and settle them down somewhere." Robert folded his arms while saying, so you picked Florida huh. It's a beautiful state I love the beaches." James kind of looked away from Robert as he said, "actually man my wife and kids were born in Florida." I've been living in the state for some years." Robert put both hands on his waist and shook his head again. James why are you hiding from your own family man? James looked at his brother and simply said, "Don't want to talk about it man, let it rest." Robert's house was sitting off a canal that spilled out into the ocean. He built his own dock to hold his boat. He supplies seafood to a few local restaurants. They both love fishing and being out on the ocean. They walked out to the boat started talking about fishing and forgot their family issues. The children were enjoying playing with their young cousins. Little James wasn't too happy playing with a five-year-old boy and girls. He much rather hang with older boys so he could learn new things to do. He really wasn't comfortable meeting new people even if it was family. Most times the kids would make fun of him when they found out he couldn't read or write at the age of eight. It was even more embarrassing when they learned he was still wetting the bed. Most of the time he would go to a corner to himself hoping no one would notice him. Sasha was busy playing with the baby she did not notice Jr. in the corner keeping to himself. Sasha was the only one who could get Jr. to come out and play. She was six but thanks to Shannon she has been reading and writing since two; she knew how to make him feel like he belonged. She promised him she would not let the other kids bully him while she was around. But getting Jr. to defend himself was proving to be useless, he'd run every time. By the time Sasha noticed him in the corner the adults were coming back in the house. They were going to have dinner here with Uncle Robert. Shannon and Sasha were happy to hear that, they were not too eager to eat greasy food tonight. Barbara would cook in someone else's kitchen; she just did not like cooking for her kids. If she didn't burn the food, it had too much salt and pepper in it. Most times she wouldn't cook at all; she'd open a can of pork and beans leave it on the table with a spoon it. But she and James would eat at the restaurant. Pricilla on the other hand was an excellent cook who loves cooking for her family, everything was made from scratch. After dinner Shannon went in the kitchen and asked her auntie if would teach her to cook good food like her. Pricilla looked at Shannon smiled and said, "Yes, come by tomorrow and I'll start you out on something easy." After saying goodbye James took his family home. As usual Shannon got the little ones ready for bed, James and Barbara was getting ready to hit the clubs in town. She has been taking care of her brother and sister since she was four. She is ten and tired of taking care of children. Often, she would daydream about being a part of a normal family having fun like a kid. She didn't hate her siblings; she just wanted to know what it's like growing up as a child not an adult. Shannon sat on the edge of the bed looking towards Sasha and Jr. wishing she was somewhere else. Sasha looked up at Shannon to see if she would tell them a story. Shannon knew that meant Sasha knows her parents are not home, and she is scared. Shannon's stories were fun to listen to. Her imagination of being in a good family playing games they were not able to play was entertaining to Sasha. The imaginary trips to places they always wanted to go would make Sasha forget about her fears and fall fast asleep. Telling the stories only made Shannon hate her life with her parents even more.

Monday morning Barbara got all three kids up early to get them registered into school. None of the kids liked going to a new school, it meant kids bullying you because you're new. For Shannon it would mean more responsibility with Sasha starting first grade. That's one more person she would have to make sure the clothes are washed and ironed. Barbara didn't care how the children looked for school she just wanted them out of the house away from her. She would often tell them she hated them and wished she never had them. She'd often say to Shannon, "My life would be better if you kids were not in it." Her neighbor from down the street was taking them. She met Joyce at the club over the weekend, found out they lived on the same street not far from each other, a new friendship began. Joyce loves being a mother but was not a faithful wife. Her husband's job always had him traveling so he was never home. She loved her husband, but she was a lonely woman with needs to be met. After making sure Barbara registered the children; Joyce talked her into taking them shopping for new clothes. She noticed Shannon was wearing clothes that didn't fit any more; she was tall for a ten-year-old. Barbara hated shopping for the kids that's wasting money she can't spend on herself. Joyce took them to her house to pick up her children. She has a house full, eight at home two living out of state. She gave the children snacks before loading them in the van. It was a treat for Barbara's children to eat a snack most of the time Barbara and James eats all the snacks from them. Shannon and Sasha were not too happy about going shopping with their mom; but since Mrs. Joyce was with them it would make it better for them. Shannon hopes it will get her clothes that fit for a change and in style. Barbara always shopped at secondhand stores because they were cheap, and she didn't feel like going store to store. Barbara hasn't been feeling like doing anything since she has entered her fifth month of pregnancy. She's also developed a strong dislike for Shannon since she grew taller and prettier. It stirs a little jealousy in her every time she looks at Shannon wishing she was young and pretty again. The ride to the mall was enough time for the kids to get to know each other. Shannon was thrilled to meet a girl her age she could talk to. She and Wanda hit it off the moment they started talking. When the van parked, they all spilled out like a never-ending water fall of children. Shannon and Sasha got scared once they got into the store; they knew the nightmare for them was about to begin. Joyce took Barb in a store that had clothes for teens seeing that Shannon was too tall for girl size. Barb went straight to the clearance rack looking for the cheapest item she could find. She doesn't care what it looks like or what size it is she is not spending a lot of money for it. Shannon held her head down as tears start rolling down her face when she sees her mom slapping hangers together at the clearance rack. Joyce noticed her and went over to see what was wrong. "You're alright Shannon?" With her head down she moans, "No." Joyce lifts her head up and asks, "What's wrong sweetie? One of my kids did something to you?" Shannon was afraid to answer that would cause a whole new scene in itself if her mom knew she was talking about her. She brushed it off and decided to tell it. "My mom doesn't know how to shop for me Mrs. Joyce. She always embarrasses me by making me try on clothes that are ugly and too small." More tears started flowing from her eyes. Joyce hugged her while rubbing her on the back saying, "There, there it's going to be okay." She didn't know what else to say to Shannon the statement took her by surprise. She looks over and saw Barbara picking all sorts of ugly items from the rack. "Stay here sweetie let me handle this." Joyce walked over to Barb, "Hey, find anything good on sale?" Barb faked a smile and said, "Oh, a little bit." Joyce looked closely at the items in her hand and asked, "So who are those for, you?" She pointed at the hideous looking blouse, odd shaped dress with a pair of pants that didn't fit either of her kids. Barb looked at the items and said, "Oh, these are for Shannon." She turned and walked over to another sales rack. Joyce stretched her eyes wide in disbelief. She was trying to think of a good way to tell Barb those were not clothes for a ten-year-old. "Barb honey, this is the women's clearance rack. You need to be in the junior department for clothes to fit Shannon." Barb looked up and saw the sign with the word women on it in big bold letters. She let out a loud sigh and put the clothes back. She was about to get mad at Joyce but realized she was right. She fake smiled it off and said, "Girl I didn't notice what area I was in I just saw clearance." They walked over to the junior area where the clothes were nice and trendy. Barb liked the area because the prices were cheaper than in the women's. Although she wasn't particular about spending money on her kids the prices were okay for her. She just started pulling clothes off the rack until she had an arm full. Before Joyce could say anything, Barb grabbed Shannon and headed for the fitting room. Shannon was not looking forward to going in there, that's where the drama would begin. Sasha took her position under a clothes rack where no one would see her. She did not want to be affiliated with what was about to happen. Barb handed Shannon a few out fits to try on, to Shannon's surprise they fit and looked good on her. She came out the fitting room smiling and loving the outfit she had on. She completely forgot she was with her mom until the slap on the head brought her back to reality. "Ouch, what you hit me for now?" she whined. Barb looked at Shannon with an angry frown; her teeth clinched together she said, "I hope you don't think I'm going to buy something like that to make you look good. Take that smile off your face before I knock it off." Shannon stopped smiling because she decided today, she is putting an end to being embarrassed by this hateful woman. Before she could say anything in defiance Joyce walks over. "Wow, Shannon that looks really nice on you, turn around. Put a smile on your face shopping isn't that bad, now try something else on for me." Shannon gladly goes back in as Joyce says to Barb, "I just love dressing little girls up, they are just too cute for words; don't you think?" She looks over at Barb who is not looking too happy at all. She managed to say an unenthused, "Yeah, it's alright." Joyce calls her girls over to try on their out fits. It eased the tension in the air until Sasha started trying on clothes. Nothing fits because she was too small for one size and too big for the other. Barb's voice got louder and louder as frustration was getting the best of her and being pregnant wasn't making her any nicer. Joyce went over to let her know she was getting too loud. Barb turned and snapped at her, "You don't tell me what to do, these are my children!" She said it with so much anger and rage, it made the wig on her head shake loosely side to side. Sasha ran under the clothes rack again, this time crying. Firmly Joyce said, "I am not trying to tell you what to do with your kids. But if you don't quiet down, you're going to get us thrown out of this store. So, stop this foolishness right now!" Barb yells back, "We'll let them throw us out, I didn't want to come here in the first place!"

Joyce looks around and see Shannon crying, she knows Sasha is hiding somewhere. Little James is on the floor laughing at his mom's wig. This is like a nightmare happening in real life. "OH God what have I gotten myself into, this woman is crazy", Joyce says to herself. She sees why Shannon hates shopping with her mom. Barb throws the rest of the clothes on the floor and storms out leaving her kids behind. Joyce couldn't believe what just happened. She looked around and saw the older kids putting the clothes back on the racks. At first, she was undecided about what to do next; but after seeing the children were okay, she continued her shopping. She bought Barb's kids a few outfits; it's the least she could do considering what happened to them. They got to the car and discovered Barb was not there. Wanda leaned over to her mom and whispered, "Where do you think she went mom?" Joyce looked at Sasha and Shannon then whispered back, "I don't know but they're not missing her." Out loud she said, "Let's get you guys something to eat and then we'll go see a movie." The children were happy about going to see a movie. Shannon and her siblings had never been out to see a movie, so it was something new for them. Joyce was afraid to think about what was going on with Barb and her children. She was afraid she would uncover something horrible. Her gut was telling her something was very wrong with this family; but she was not the one to dig up somebody else dirt, she has dirt of her own to keep hid. Barbara made it home with no concern at all about her children, besides nobody was going to make her spend her money. She walked home from the mall; her fast-long strides got her there quick. Barb is not mentally stable or fit to be raising children. Being bipolar with epilepsy is something she has managed to hide from others. It doesn't take much to send her in a mental whirlwind, especially when things don't go the way she wants it. Her mind kept repeating the same thing over and over, nobody tells me what to do. She was huffing her way down the street like a raging bull. As she entered the house she began pacing back and forth talking to herself. She was getting more and angrier trying to think of someone to blame besides herself for her actions. "I didn't want children, they made me get married." They are her parents; she always blames them when she deals with children. Her parents had a horrible house fire that destroyed everything they had including taking the lives of three children. Barbara was the youngest at the time of the fire. She was rescued and thrown out the window with half her body on fire. Her head hit a rock as she landed on the ground. The other three children could not be saved. Her mom often would say her daughter died in that fire with the others, she acts nothing like the child she knew. She was different in a bad way. She continued to pace back and forth talking to the voices in her head. "Somebody is going to pay; nobody tells me what to do."

After the movie Joyce took the kids to her house for dinner. There were too many of them to take out to eat. It was cheaper to cook at home. Shannon was just happy not being around her mom, she never likes going home. She knows her mom is going to blame her for what happened today, she always does. Shannon wishes she could just run away to a better family; to be in a home where parents love and protect their children not abuse them. "She never tells us she loves us," she mumbles. Tears fill her eyes as she looks at little James and Sasha. She closes her eyes and takes a deep breath and shook away the tears. Then a thought comes to mind, "You gotta keep it together girl for their sake." Joyce quietly walks over to Shannon and gives her a hug. Shannon asked her, "What was that for Mrs. Joyce?" She spoke to Shannon in a soft loving tone, "I felt you needed it sweetie." She gave Shannon a kiss on the forehead and went back in the kitchen. The tears wanted to come back but once again she held them in. Oh, how she longed to hear her mom speak to her with tenderness in her voice. After dinner Joyce asked the boys to walk Barb's kids' home. She found it strange that Barbara never came by to see if the children were okay, or if they were missing. She wouldn't dare think of Barb being a horrible mother; her gut was telling her something was wrong.

Shannon walked in the house first and spotted the large can of pork and beans sitting on the table with a spoon in it. That was Barbara's way of fixing them dinner, opening a cold can of whatever and putting it on the table. Junior ran over to the table jumped in the chair pulled the can close and started eating. Shannon angrily said, "Boy! What are you doing? We just ate." Junior just swallowed then said, "I'm still hungry;" then shoved another spoonful in his mouth. They heard music playing in their parents' bedroom, and Barb singing along in her horrible opera high pitched voice. Shannon shook her head as her and Sasha walked away leaving Junior at the table eating. Sasha was sleepy so Shannon had to give her a bath quickly and get her to bed. She looked at Sasha laying there looking cute as ever sleeping wondering, how could someone have kids and not love them enough to care for them. If I can just get away from here and never come back. At the thought of that tears began flowing she didn't try to stop. Sasha rolled over opened her eyes to see her sister crying. She didn't have to ask what was wrong she knew. She went over to Shannon and hugged her leg to comfort her. "It's going to be okay Shan, one day you'll be able to get away from her for good." She kneeled down to Sasha hugged her tight as they both cried for a little while. They let go and Shannon says to her little sister, "You're a good sister even though you're spoiled rotten." They giggled and cried at the same time when she said that. Sasha got back in bed as Shannon went to take her bath. Junior took his bath while they were having their sister moment of tears as he called it. Shannon came in the room to find Junior was sitting on the bed with Sasha waiting for her to tell them a story. The two were tired but they would not stay sleep until they hear a Shannon bedtime story. It started out as her imaginary life away from abusive parents but ended up helping Sasha understand reading stories in books better. She wasn't halfway through the story and the two were fast asleep. She put James in his bed then got in her bed only to lay there wishing she was someplace else. Her eyes opened to a new morning; she had no idea when she fell asleep. She was up doing a routine she felt was not fair to her being a mom to kids. Junior had wet in the bed again; something is wrong with him for him to still be doing this at his age she thought. She tries to teach junior things, but he doesn't remember anything. She told Barb Junior was not learning in school, he can't read or write. When she told her, he was still wetting in his bed, Barbara would beat him figuring she could knock some sense in him. She would just say he was pretending to be dumb and wouldn't allow the school to test him. Shannon gave up on helping him learn. She told Sasha he has a block in his head that's stopping him from learning. Sasha thinks he has a brick up there that needs to be taken out. Shannon had junior taking the linen off the bed and bathing. They put the wet mattress outside to dry in the sun. They got dressed and ran out the house heading to Uncle Robert so Aunt Priscilla can show Shannon how to cook better. By the time James and Barbara got up the kids had been gone for some time. Neither of them could care less where the children were. After looking in their rooms and not seeing them; Barbara just went to the kitchen to cook her and James some breakfast. They made it just in time to their uncle house as Priscilla was just starting to cook. Shannon and Sasha went straight to the kitchen. They were so excited about learning to cook the right way. Shannon asked Priscilla, "Auntie could you show me how to cook clean eggs?" Priscilla wasn't sure if she should answer or laugh. Before she could say anything, Sasha jumped in to explain. "Yeah Auntie, I don't want to eat mama's dirty eggs and black bacon anymore. I want some clean ones please. Do you wash yours?" Priscilla couldn't help but laugh. "What are you girls talking about? There's no such thing as dirty eggs." Sasha giggles and says in defense, "Ya huh, mama cooks them all the time when she fix us breakfast." Priscilla laughs harder thinking kids say the dandiest things; she gave up trying to explain, "Okay girls, I will teach you how to cook clean eggs and bacon. The secret is clean oil or butter if you like." She shows them the cooking oil can. Sasha is excited, "Wow Auntie, I've never seen clean oil before. Where'd you get it from?" Priscilla answered cautiously; she didn't want to send Sasha's thoughts twirling. "I got it from the grocery store. You ever go to the Grocery store with your mom?" She felt it was a safe question to ask until she got the answer. "OH no Auntie, we never go to the store with mom for food, she acts very badly if we are with her, so we always say we want to stay home." Priscilla didn't know what to say and was too afraid to ask another question. The conversation seems to be taking her where she did not want to go. She continued showing them the items they needed without any further comments on what their mom does. She let Shannon do the cooking so she would learn faster doing it hands on. She saw Shannon knew how to do everything else, so she went to dress her four little ones. Sasha and junior got to play with their cousins while they wait to eat. Little Robert was the oldest followed by Susan, Angie and baby Karen. James was glad to have a boy to play with around so many girls. Both boys went to an area away from the girls and played. They were surprised to find Aunt Sadie was there, they saw her last night. Sasha looked exactly like Sadie when she was born. That's why James spoils her; he loves his baby sister Sadie. They were happy to find that Aunt Sadie was staying there. Priscilla wasn't, her and Sadie didn't like each other for good reasons. Sadie mistreats Priscilla's kids and she won't work. But James kids Sadie loves, and she always worked when she stayed with James; only because she didn't want to piss off Barbara who she know will go crazy on her. Breakfast was ready but the table in the kitchen was too small to seat everyone, so the little ones was put on newspaper spread out on the floor to eat. Shannon cooked the grits better than her Aunt thought she could. Everybody kept going back for more until it was gone. Priscilla was glad Shannon came over for a cooking lesson she helped her clean the kitchen before and after they ate. Her kids are too small to help in the kitchen. Shannon told her how to cook her grits and Priscilla gave Shannon a small can of clean oil as they call it to take home. They spent practically the whole day with their Auntie's and cousins. Priscilla was able to get a lot of housework done without having to stop and take care of the kids. Shannon kept the children busy for her and made sure they had lunch and a thirty-minute nap time. Once Priscilla was finished with her daily chores Shannon decided it was time to leave and goes to see her friends. Priscilla thanked her and told her to come back and visit any time, she felt like she was on vacation while Shannon was with her. As they were heading to the path to get home they ran into a gang of kids. Shannon knew by looking at them they were gang members coming to defend their street from strangers. She was not going to let them touch Sasha; James was big enough to defend himself. Which for him it means scream and run away so you'll be well to run another day. The gang leader steps forward and walk around the three of them looking them over. He stops in front of Shannon and ask, "Who told ya'll to come on my strip?" The gang nods their head as to say they're in agreement with the question. Shannon slowly pushes Sasha behind her balling her hand into a fist not taking her eyes off the boy standing in front of her. No sooner as she gets Sasha safely behind her, she swings making contact under his chin, a perfect upper cup. His head snaps back and he falls to the ground. It looked like he was falling in slow motion to Shannon. Before he hit the ground, she was punching him again, his crew couldn't believe what was happening in front of them. James jumped high in the air and let out a loud scream like a girl and took off running towards home like he always does when a fight breaks out; leaving the girls to fend for themselves. No one else jumped in to help the leader; street rule is when it's one on one you wait until it's done. Aside from that they were too shocked to react to the beat down Shannon was giving their fearless leader. She kept punching him until she finally noticed he was knocked out cold. She quickly jumped up grabbed Sasha looking to see if anybody else was stepping her way; nobody moved they just stood there looking at their friend lying on the pavement. When they looked up Shannon and Sasha were gone, they were not going to hang around for another fight. Shannon didn't know that beating up the gang leader meant she was now the leader of the gang and his territory was now hers to rule, but she would soon find out. She dropped off the can of oil at the back door of their room until they come home from playing. They had fun getting to know Joyce kids better playing without being picked at. They got home just before dark as usual there was a cold can of pork and beans on the table with a large spoon in it. She was surprised to see a chicken wing on a small plate next to the beans. They always had to split one wing between the three of them. Their parents weren't home and there was no telling when they'd be back; they were used to being left home alone. Sasha was glad they ate dinner at Mrs. Joyce house; she didn't like eating the bony part of the wing. With Shannon's permission little James ate the wing and beans he was always hungry; they took a bath and went to bed. Shannon was tired from all the playing and cleaning, but it was the fight that got the best of her; she was sleep as soon as her head hit the pillow. There was five weeks of summer left to enjoy before school starts. After eating breakfast, they went to Joyce house to hang out with Wanda and her siblings. It was there Shannon found out she was the new gang leader of her Uncle Robert's street. Later she had to fight for the right to hang out on her own street. The bully was the girl who lived next door to Shannon. She was the same age tall with beautiful dark black velvet skin, her name is Gwen. Shannon thought to herself, "This is why I hate moving so much. You always have to prove to some dumb kid you belong somewhere; I hate my life." Gwen had been watching Shannon from her window since they moved in. She was waiting for the right moment to introduce herself to the new kid. Since she heard the new kid beat up the guy two streets over, she needs to let her know who rules this one. She called Shannon to come out in the street to fight her for the right to be there. Shannon went out and stood at the edge of the yard where Gwen was standing; nothing was said at first as they circled looking each other over. When they stopped Shannon threw the first punch, but Gwen didn't go down; she knew it was going to be a tough fight. All the children came running to cheer them on; really hoping to get a new leader. No one liked Gwen but nobody could beat her.

The two fought until they were too tired to pass another punch; it was called a truce until they decide to fight again. Two days later they met again when Shannon came storming out the house mad about her mom being pregnant again; it meant things were getting worse for her. She doesn't want to take care of another baby; she just wants to be a kid. As Shannon made her way to a yard of black dirt Gwen approached her, they circled then the fists were flying. Both girls ended up lying out in the dirt tapping each other calling it a hit; they finally called it a truce and decided to share the street. This means if anyone wanted to challenge for the street, they had to fight them both for it. At first Shannon didn't like being a gang leader. Every time she would come out the house the kids would gather around her. There were some perks to it that she liked though; if she said she had a taste for some peanuts and a soda. Someone would run up to the store and get it for her, and she didn't have to fight to fit in. Of course, the gang from the other street was happy. They finally get to come two streets over and hang with the snooty kids. All the houses on the street were big brick houses, but two streets over the houses were small wooden ones that were closer to the canal that ran through. Some were old built on stilts leaning. Others didn't look to be in livable condition, but people lived in them trying to make it with what they had.

The summer was a hot one and at the end of Shannon's street was a rundown graveyard that was next to the train tracks with trusses over the canal. The canal leads out to the ocean; the water is not always high, there are days when it's very shallow. Shannon wanted to see what the canal was like because the other guys would talk about how they would swim in it during hot summer days. They all gathered together to go for a swim in the canal. They had to pass through the small graveyard to get to the water; it was overgrown with tall weeds and grass. There were a few pretty flowers and shaded trees that looked like claws reaching down at you at night. Only a few grave plots had fresh flowers on them; some family members were keeping the area around them clean. They reached the canal and found the water was still high enough to swim in. Everyone came prepared to swim except Sasha, she was afraid of water getting in her face. She would get seasick from looking at the water waves from dry land. She sat at the top of the embankment watching the kids have fun. The teenage boys decided to walk along the trusses to see how far back the tracks went. It stretched across the widest part of the canal; the swimming hole was on the narrow end. They were getting close to the trusses end on the other side when they heard the train coming around the bend. Instead of running towards the end they turned around and started running back the way they came. The conductor spotted the boys running just as the train cleared the bend and started blowing the whistle; the boys started screaming and running even faster to try and reach an opening on the trusses in the middle of the canal where they could jump off. The kids in the water swimming got out and ran up the embankment to see the train go over the water. When they saw the boys running in front of the train everybody started yelling run, run. Two of the boy's sisters started crying as the train was quickly approaching the boys. There were sparks coming from the wheels as the conductor was trying his best to slow the trains speed. Then everyone started screaming, "Jump, jump!" Horrified by what was about to happen before their eyes. The train was gaining on them fast; the conductor by this time had the whistle blaring loudly urging the boys to move faster. He didn't want his train to hit and kill the boys. He leaned out the small window and started yelling, "Run, please run faster." His heart was beating so fast and hard from fear it felt like it was about to come out of his chest. Tears started welling in his eyes as the train was almost nipping at the boy's heels. The boys jumped before the train could hit them. He screamed a nervous shaky "Yes", then quickly regrouped his emotions and angrily yelled through the small window, "Damn bad ass kids!" The train slowly continues its run on the track to its destination. The boys hit the water and began swimming to shore. High on adrenaline they get out of the water and lay on the sand breathing hard from the run of their lives. Darren who is seventeen looks up at the train passing and say, "We were lucky I'll never do that again." The other two boys' knees were shaking so bad they couldn't stand up if they tried. They looked at where they jumped from and said, "Burr" shivering with fear as they lay back on the sand. All the children ran over to them feeling both excited and scared. The girls were asking through tears of relief, are you guys alright? What were you thinking doing something like that? Were you scared? Before they could answer the boys came up cheering. "Woe, man that was awesome! You guys played chicken with a train, man that was super crazy! "All the boys started laughing like it was the best prank ever done, but deep down inside they were scared out of their wits; they didn't want the girls to know that. Going along with the rest of the gang the three boys put on their brave face and laughed it off too. The girls stopped crying and looked at the boys laughing. They got angry at the boys and said, "Ya'll boys play too much, that was not funny. Ya'll scare the crap out of us. Ugh! Ya'll just play too much!" As the girls walked away, the boys gathered in closer together for a moment of serious evaluation of what just happened. Stan decided to ask first, "Are you guys alright? Man, that was a crazy serious stunt ya'll pulled off." Nobody was laughing as Darren answered, "Man I thought I was going to die up there. I thought I was going to die." Chuck was finally able to talk after being choked with fear, "Shit man that was some intense run of fear. I was so scared I didn't know what to think." Tate sat up saying, "YO, I was running so hard my ears started ringing." Darren pushed Tate down and said, "Man that wasn't your ears that was the train whistle blowing out our ear drums." Tate sat up and asked, "What train whistle?" They all just laughed but was surprised to hear Tate say, "Man I want to do that again." They all shook their heads saying Tate you crazy, let's go have some safe fun." They met up with the other kids but wasn't in the mood to get back in the water. The weeds were too high around the graveyard to do anything else, so they decided to go home early they had enough excitement for the day. The next two weeks was spent going back and forth showing Shannon her new territory. She had them all getting along like family; with so many kids hanging around Shannon and Gwen was creating crazy things to do to keep them out of trouble; they would even help the boys prank the girls for a good laugh. After finding out they were stealing to get her whatever she asked for, a few of them started doing honest chores around the neighborhood to earn cash for whatever she needed; the main meeting house was at Mrs. Joyce with her permission. Joyce and her husband had ten kids and they love to entertain. The house was one of the biggest on the street, seven bedrooms and four and a half baths with a pool. The family room had a wet bar for adult entertainment which happens twice a month during the summer. She would give the kids a pool party on Wednesday and Saturday afternoon. Wanda was Joyce second of three girls; Tisha was the baby girl but not the last born. Wanda and Shannon became best friends at first sight. Shannon liked hanging with the gang she felt safe and everyone treated her like she was important. It was not like that at home. Barbara was starting to show she was pregnant, which meant less time going out to the bars. Her being home more was an increase of aggravation for Shannon who started spending more time at Joyce house to escape. Barbara didn't care where the children went as long as they were away from her. During the morning they would go spend time with Priscilla. Shannon loved helping her aunt with her kids, plus her aunt was teaching her how to dress and fix her hair better. On Wednesday they would leave early to go to the pool party that Joyce was having for them. Their cousins couldn't come because Uncle Robert wouldn't allow them to leave the house. All the kids came over to swim; even the teen gangs came after calling a truce and joining with the teen gang on the street. Joyce had plenty of food and drinks for them. There were plenty of games for them to play in the yard, but they all stayed in and around the pool. No one else had a pool at their house, so it was all about swimming for them. The teens started playing dare games having so much fun until the little ones gathered around them. Little James wanted to join in on the hotdog eating dare, but Shannon wouldn't let him. He whined about it until she went in the house with Wanda to get out of the sun. By then the boys came up with the peanut butter dare; who can swallow the most peanut butter on a spoon? Little James looked around to see if Shannon had come back out yet, no sign of her. He went over to try and join in on the fun. At first, they wouldn't let him in on the dare it was for big boys only they told him. But James kept bugging them and yelled out, "I can eat a table spoon full!" They looked at him in silence; finally, someone said, "I dare ya." Another one said, "I double dare ya." James grabbed the big spoon and dipped it in the jar and pulled it out with a big glob of peanut butter on it. Darren went up to him and said, "Little man don't do it that's too much." Tate shouted out, "I triple dog dare ya!" "Oooohhh," Everybody chimed at once. Darren knew Tate was up to no good with his dare, but before he could take the spoon from James, he had already put it in his mouth. Darren yelled at James with panic in his voice, "Boy I told you not to do that!" Then he realized James was choking, his eyes stretched wide with fear and his mouth open trying to heave up the peanut butter to no avail. Tears start rolling down his face as he put his hands to his throat to try and push the lump up. Darren grabs him and hits him on his back to jar the lump loose, nothing. James is getting weak and limp as his eyes are starting to roll back, he's about to pass out. All the children are in a state of panic except Tate; he's laughing as if he's enjoying himself seeing James suffer. Wanda brother Michael runs over to James and punches him in the stomach; the lump shoots out and splatters on the pavement. James falls to his knees coughing and gasping for air. His eyes are red and full of tears as he sits down to take in as much air as he could and starts crying. His heart is beating fast from the fear of dying. The oldest brother Gary picks James up to calm him down, "You going to be alright little man." Gary and Michael are home visiting for a couple of weeks, they miss being with the family from time to time, so they come home. Gary is a pro boxer living in New York, Michael is studying law. He walks over and rubs James head soothing him, then turned and saw Tate laughing leaning on the wall. Before anyone could say anything, Michael went up to Tate slapped him so hard on his head, Tate fell over the patio table and rolled onto the concrete. Michael stood over him enraged with anger pointed his finger in Tate's face and said, "That shit isn't funny you crazy ass fool. That little boy could have died!" Tate grinned a little looking up at Mike as he was about to bend down and pop him with his fist to wipe the grin off his face. Gary grabbed Mike saying, "It's not worth it man, little dude is okay now let's go." The other children were too shock to speak, some were exhaling from holding their breath. Sasha was crying because she just knew her brother wasn't going to make it out of this one; she felt so helpless. Shannon came out of the house in time to see Gary rescue James. She was scared and mad at James at the same time; she told him not to play big boys' games. In a sense maybe that'll teach him to listen she thought. She turned around and saw Tate lift himself off the patio. She was perplexed by the way he was acting watching James suffocate on a lump of peanut butter; he was amused at watching her brother die. She was beginning to feel that something was going wrong inside Tate's head. She decided to talk to Darren about his friend; Tate is beginning to be too dangerous to be around the younger kids. Tate notice Shannon is looking at him, he shrugs his shoulder at her and walks away. Tate's crew is starting to wonder about him themselves. They jokingly call him crazy, now he's starting to act like he really is crazy. Darren knows Tate better than anybody they've been friends since four. Darren's the leader of the crew two streets over, when he heard Shannon took the streets from the small brotherhood, he had to meet her. When he heard what street she lived on, he decided to negotiate a truce with the crew leader on her street. It was his way of getting them in the hood of the upper class living as they called it. It was a well-kept middle class to upper middle-class neighborhood. Both areas are clean now thanks to Shannon, she is now teaching the gang to read better. Hanging in this neighborhood has changed Darren's outlook on life for himself. Looking at his friend life fall to pieces and his mind deteriorate is not making him feel good. Seeing Tate take joy out of seeing someone about to die has Darren worried.

James was in the house sleeping on the sofa in the den. Tate left after everybody got on him for coaxing James into that challenge knowing he was too young. Wanda's eighteen-year-old brother David runs the crew in the hood; he walks over to Darren to warn him, "I'm going to say this once, keep Tate in line or I'll do it for ya. Your man is loose in the head." They both looked towards the road and walked away from each other with nothing else needing to be said. The smaller kids continued to play in the pool once they knew James was alright. It was a fun day for Shannon, best pool party she's ever been to. It's the first time she felt like she belongs to something important, now it's time to go home. Friday David and Darren had a secret meeting to discuss Tate. Darren told David about Tate's troubled life. Tate's mom is always high on drugs; he's taking care of her more than she is him. His dad abuses him for everything his mom doesn't do. He beats him with whatever is in his hand; belt, boot, extension cord, pots whatever. His dad is a truck driver he's rarely home, but when he is Tate gets the brunt of the violence from both parents. After hearing Tate's situation David went from anger to intervention mode. He realized Tate was at the point of seriously hurting himself or someone else. He's a good kid in a bad situation, coming up with a way to get Tate to redirect the violence boiling inside of him will have to be handled with care if it's not too late already. They agreed shook hands and said, "Family, let's take care of our own."

Shannon, Wanda and Gwen got all the children together to teach them to read and do math. Summer will be over in less than two weeks. Most of the children from the other street couldn't read. As bad as Gwen is, she's pretty smart, she's the only child her parents have. Joyce loved having the children teach at her house, she found out Shannon was smarter than the average ten-year-old. She should be in high school. Six-year-old Sasha was too advanced for her age. Joyce thought, Barbara has some intelligent little girls, but she is not too bright herself. She wanted to tell Barb her girls were in grade levels that was below their level. But she has learned never go to Barb about her children; that's like opening a whole new kind of Pandora box. Joyce shook the thought of that off and said, "Oh no! Not going to deal with that again once is enough for me." She laughed to herself then went to fix the kids some snacks. Shannon had Sasha helping with reading stories out loud to the kids. It will be Sasha's first time going to the big school with Shannon and James. Shannon wanted to make sure her little sister would be ready for school and not have to struggle like she did when she started. The problem is Sasha doesn't know she has learned lessons above her grade level; she's been doing it since she was two. Shannon acts very mature for a ten-year-old; but when you must take care of two kids like you're their parents it has a tendency of making you grow up quick, fast and in a hurry. She doesn't complain about taking care of them; she just complains that no one is taking care of her.

David and Darren got to the house and saw the playroom was full of children doing schoolwork both big and small. He smiled at Shannon with approval on how a little girl could have such a positive influence on a bunch of hood rats. Some of Darren's crew was sitting in learning how to read finally. Shannon had a way of making learning fun and easy. Since all was well with the crew, David and Darren left the scene to go hook up with Tate. They were on a mission to defuse a ticking time bomb in a friend. After Shannon dismissed class, they ate dinner at Joyce then went home. They took a bath and went to bed early. Saturday morning came fast thanks to Barb, she woke the kids up at five that morning to clean the mess she made cooking her and James Sr. dinner. They were well rested and full of energy at five in the morning going to bed early paid off. The three of them had to clean the kitchen. Barbara later sent Shannon and Sasha to clean the bathroom while she deals with little James bed wetting. She was fed up with him pissing up her good linen. Her method for getting him to stop clearly was not working. She would scream and yell at him, "you stank, you stank," while beating him on the head. She figured if she hit on his head enough it would knock some sense in him. It didn't change anything, but she felt good knowing that she beat him for it. Shannon and Sasha would comfort him after Barb would leave the room. They felt sorry for their brother; they knew he couldn't stop wetting the bed even though he was trying not to. He made an effort to get up with Sasha during the night to use the bathroom but would still wake up soak and wet. After the beatings he would have knots on his little arms from protecting his head, Shannon would rub them down with green alcohol. They sat down to breakfast after the torture and cleaning was done, only to end up cleaning again. There were no watching cartoons on Saturday morning for them, Barb wasn't having it. The only ones watching TV in the house was her and James Sr. After the kitchen was cleaned again Barb had the children washing laundry until noon. By then she was tired of looking at them in the house with her, she made them go outside to play. Her stomach was getting bigger; she was getting cranky as the children were getting on her nerves. She can't wait for school to start none of them will be home with her. Shannon and a few kids went to hang out at Wanda's house. They wanted to go play at the canal rather than be around the pool. Joyce was not letting them go without the older ones being there with them. Dave came in ten minutes after Shannon, before Wanda could whine him into taking them. Joyce let him know what the deal was and let him decide if he wanted the little ones at the canal with them. The teenagers were always at the canal, but since Shannon had the little ones cleaning the neighborhood the teenagers joined in. Since the train no one has been at the canal. Dave gathered the crew and went over the rules with the little ones and off they went. They could barely see the water in the canal as they approached it. Darren went down to see how deep the water was. He went towards the middle the water only came up to his knees. He yelled up to them saying, "Definitely no diving." As he came to the top of the embankment, he finished saying his assessment, "The little ones can safely splash in it." Wanda and Shannon were happy to hear they could at least sit in the water. Sasha was able to come down to the water without getting sick. Some of the older boys started throwing rocks making them skim across the water. David had most of the crew cleaning the weeds and overgrowth around the graveyard. They decided this would be their summer hang out. They chopped down tree limbs in a corner not far from the canal, cut the grass and made it a picnic area. They were all enjoying themselves beautifying their spot. The little ones moved further down to watch the rock skimming contest between the boys.

David, Darren and Tate began clearing the area taking the tree limbs to the side of the road for trash pickup. They plan to take a break and watch the others as soon as the debris is cleaned up. But disaster strikes in the midst of them before they know it. Tate dropped the limbs he had in his arms turned around and started running towards the canal screaming. Darren was near the road too far away to grab him. He yelled at David, "get him, get him!" David lunged to tackle him but missed. Tate dove in headfirst into the canal. Silence fell over the area for a few seconds that seemed like minutes as they all watch in disbelief as the horror unfolds in front of them. No one paid attention to the big rock in the canal until Tate's head slammed into it. SPLASH! His neck snapped and body started twitching splashing the water. Everybody started running out of the water screaming and crying. Darren took off running to the water to his friend hoping he was alive. He slid down the embankment and splashed his way to

Tate's lifeless body. He grabbed him, sat down and held him close as tears began flowing down his face. Rocking back and forth he began saying, "why did you do this? You said you were okay!" He kept repeating it over and over. The little ones scattered running home to get the adults. Joyce called the emergency units first before any of the others because her house was the first to get the news. All the parents in the hood made it to the canal before the policemen. They had been trying to no avail to get Darren to come out of the water. It took a while, but they had to sedate him to calm him down. He was covered in blood as they guided him out of the water. He was taken to the hospital for observation, but they all knew that meant he would be in the crazy ward. The police questioned all the children to find out what happened. Some were not able to talk from crying screaming so much. A few of the teenagers were able to tell what happened clearly. Everyone cleared the area quickly; it was too much for the children to hang around any longer. Aside from the tragedy the adults did notice the clean-up the children did to the area. The graveyard looked like a peaceful resting place again. They all went home hurt and confused by what happened. Tate's mother was on her way to get her next fix when she got the news of her son's death. The last few days of summer were spent healing a broken community. The streets were quiet for days in both neighborhoods. No children were out doing anything until the day of the funeral. The community came together and collected money to help pay for the funeral. Tate's parents decided to bury him in the graveyard by the canal. A tomb stone was donated by a stranger to mark the final resting place. Darren had to be admitted into a mental institution; he went crazy and was not able to deal with his friend's death. Tate's mom Claire would visit the grave site every day all day. She no longer wanted the drugs only the love of a child she no longer had. She had not noticed she no longer wanted a fix; she would sit at the grave and cry for hours saying nothing.

CHAPTER TWO

The first week of school is always the most exciting; kids get to show off new clothes, form new groups to hang with. Shannon is happy because for the first time she is not starting school being bullied for being the new kid. She has a lot of friends who have her back should anyone start a fight with her. They all walk to school together except for the children Sasha's age; they have to catch a bus; the district doesn't want kids under second grade walking to school. There wasn't much chatter going on the way to school, they were all still getting over what Tate did. Thanks to Shannon many of them are going back to school reading, they can't wait to show what they learned during the summer. Sasha is scared being in a big school with so many people she doesn't know. She stood on the sidewalk near the bus ramp by herself waiting for Shannon to come to school. She knew where her class was, but she didn't know the students in her class. Different teachers would come up to her and offer to take her to her class; but she would tell them she is waiting for her big sister to come and take her. Finally, she sees the gang coming towards the school. She was brave the whole while she was standing there by herself waiting for Shannon; but the moment she saw her big sister she started crying. She had never gone anywhere without Shannon by her side. Shannon saw Sasha crying in the distance and ran to her to ask why she wasn't in class. Sasha hugged Shannon tight crying telling her she wanted to wait for her to take her to class. Shannon realized it was the first time Sasha was not with her, so calming her down she walked Sasha to her class. She told Sasha from now on wait for her outside the class and she will not take so long getting to school. At first Sasha wouldn't go in the classroom full of strangers, but Shannon assured her she was going to be okay. She pointed to the end of the hall and said, "Just come up those stairs and you'll see me in my class if you need me. Not everybody knows each other on the first day Sasha, so don't be afraid." Shannon cleaned the tears from Sasha's face and watched her slowly walk in and take a seat. When she looked back at the door Shannon was gone and she felt alone again. She sat at a desk close to the door and looked around at all the other children. She noticed she was the smallest in the class, still the height of a four-year-old. She was used to being the smallest at home; it's scary being the smallest around strangers. All the kids in class were mixing and mingling playing games together except Sasha, she just sat and watched them talk and play. The teacher came in just as the final bell rang for class to start. She called the class to order and introduced herself to them. "Good morning class, my name is Mrs. Vinegar and I would like to welcome you to your first day of school. The first thing we are going to do is get to know each other so we won't be strangers. When I point at you please stand and say your name loud and clear so the class will know who you are; okay, let's began." One by one she points to each student to say their name. Sasha was feeling really scared as it was getting close to being her turn. Finally, the moment came for her; she stood up and nervously said her name then quickly sat back down. The class was looking around trying to see who was speaking; they could barely see her head above the desktop. Some of them started asking, what was the name? Who said that? The teacher called her to the front of the class and asked her to say her name one more time so the class could see and hear her. Sasha wanted to hide but the teacher gestured for her to come forward. She slowly made her way to the front hoping no one would laugh at her for being small. Mrs. Vinegar looked down at her and said, "Oh my, aren't you a tiny one." Before Sasha could say her name the teacher was introducing her, "Class this is Sasha." She kneeled down to Sasha to ask, "Are you supposed to be in school? You don't look a day over four; how old are you Sasha? Fear left Sasha as it upset her that the teacher thought she was four. Speaking proper and politely she answered, "Yes Mrs. Vinegar I'm old enough to be in school I am six years old." The teacher frowned a little at the fact that the little girl spoke proper, and then faked a smile as she told Sasha to take her seat. Sasha noticed the frown and suspected the teacher didn't like her because she was short. I'll just tell Shannon she'll know what to do, she thought as she made her way back to her desk.

Little James class was behind Sasha's; his day started out okay until the teacher found out he was left-handed. It didn't go well for him from that time on. His teacher did not want him writing with his left. She would hit his left to force him to use the right hand that he couldn't write at all with. He couldn't understand why it was wrong for him use his left hand. The teacher kept yelling at him "writing with the left means mentally handicapped, you will not be handicapped in my class." James gave up and ran to the corner crying looking out the window wishing he was home. His first day is turning out to be a nightmare. The teacher's method is cruel but perhaps she is on to something concerning James mental state of mind. He does have a problem remembering how to read and write.

Shannon's class was on the second floor with the sixth to eighth graders. It was the new building added to the school. None of the kids from the hood was in her class so far. Wanda was in the class next door; she could see her through the glass wall that separated the two classes. The outside of the building was brick, but inside was glass boxes. The halls were very wide with marble floors shining like glass. The eighth graders were on the first floor of the new building. Shannon's teacher was a young beautiful twenty-five-year-old blond hair blue eye with a body that turned heads of many men and boys. Jealous women stared hating wishing they had her package. Of course, she knew she looked good and she loved the attention. The moment she saw Shannon walk in her class; she knew she would have to share that attention. Shannon was a tall thin pretty girl who could pass for a teenager because of her height. With her smooth light brown skin complexion and infectious smile, her personality commanded attention; but her innocence was breath taking. No woman can compete with innocence she thought as she was filled with anger just looking at Shannon. She knew it was silly of her to feel that way about a little girl but feels this one is a threat to her image. She shook it off for the time being to start the class. "Good morning class, my name is Miss Belinda I want you stand and tell me your name so I can put a face to the name I have in my book starting from the left." One by one they stood up saying their names until the last person was done. Shannon felt confident about the start of this school year because she wasn't being treated like the new kid for a change. But there is a new girl in class that the kids are laughing at because her clothes are dirty and wrinkle. Shannon didn't laugh because she knows how it feels. She recalls the girl saying her name was Eddy Gal, she could pass for white, but she talked like she's black. She was dirty and smelly with brownish blond hair frizzy and tangled. Barbara use to send Shannon to school like that until Shannon learned how to take care of herself from her big sister Louise. She is now teaching Sasha what Louise taught her. Shannon looks back at Eddy as she raises her hand to get the teacher attention. Miss Belinda acknowledges her looks in the book for the name, "Yes Eddy, you have a question?" Eddy hesitates for a moment then finally ask; "May I go to the bathroom please?" Miss Belinda looks at her disgusted by the sight of the child answers, "Yes, please go." The class giggles as Eddy makes her way to the door only to stop and turn to say; "Excuse me Miss Belinda, I don't where it is." Before Belinda could respond Shannon stood up and said, I'll show her where it is Miss Belinda." She waves them off with her hand to go. Shannon rushes Eddy out the door and heads down the hall to the bathroom. Wanda saw them pass by her class, so she raised her hand to be dismissed to go too. They were quiet until they got in the bathroom then

Eddy admits she didn't have to use it she only wanted to get out of class. She was tired of the kids laughing at her. Wanda walks in, "So what's going on Shannon? Who's the new girl?" Shannon answer, "Her name is Eddy Gal; then turns to Eddy and say, "I use to do the same thing. Since we are in here though we may as well get you looking and smelling better." They showed her how to use paper towels and hand soap to bathe with. They even put some soap in her hair to somewhat get it to smell good. Wanda pulled a comb out of her purse so they could do her hair; yep they turned the bathroom into a spa hair salon. There wasn't anything they could do about the dirty wrinkled dress but at least she didn't smell bad. Eddy looked in the mirror with teary eyes she turned to them and said, "Thank you guys so much, and I've never looked this good before." They giggled as she hugged them both then the three left the bathroom to go back to class. Eddy's head was held high with a smile on her face as they walked down the hall. She didn't care about the dirty clothes; her hair was pretty and smelled clean. The class was taken by the change in Eddy's attitude when she walked back to her desk. They couldn't help but notice her face, hands and knees were clean, and her hair was neat too. Shannon walked to her desk smiling thinking to herself, wow there was a pretty girl under all that dirt; then giggled out loud. Miss Belinda looked at Eddy and sneered then said, "Hum." She rolled her eyes and frowned up her lips at Shannon then turned her attention to the rest of the class. She decided to give a quiz to find out what her students retained over the summer. By the end of the day she found the students this year was pretty smart, no slow ones to hold the class back. But to her surprise Shannon was smarter than any of the ten-year-old she should be in high school with advanced lessons.

Finally, the day was done school is out as the bell rings to dismiss classes. The children came running out like a herd of cattle during a stampede. They all had a hand full of papers for parents to read and or sign. Everybody was happy except little James, but he listened to them bragging about the cool games and lessons learned. Shannon introduced Eddy to Gwen and the gang; they were surprised to learn she stayed across from Wanda. It seemed impossible to them because they thought the house was abandoned and haunted. There were no lights or water on but there were always noise coming from the house, now they know who were making the noise. Eddy assured them she lived in the house with her other seven siblings; she is number three of ten. Eddy told Shannon and Wanda her parents were never home with them long; they were home to buy food for them then leave; it was the only time the lights and water were on. The food would run out long before their parents return back home. Shannon and Wanda understood why she came to school dirty. Wanda wanted to tell her to come over and bathe at her house but that was too many children she decided to talk to her mom about it first. Shannon was never without lights and water Barbara just didn't care to do anything for her kids. Shannon told Eddy how to put clothes under the mattress to get the wrinkles out. Gwen and Wanda burst out laughing to here such a thing. But Shannon reminded them of how she looked when she first moved in their house. They quickly stopped laughing and thought for a minute then said, "oh yeah, you're right, WOW! Well who knew?" They were sounding like a choir speaking at the same time, the four of them laughed as Shannon said, "Ya'll so silly." They all went home with fresh new names to remember from school. The first week of school past by quickly, all the papers were signed, and fees were paid. Parents were not happy about the extra fees and new field trips being added, that means paying more money for them. They are angry about in the beginning of the year, but they're not going to think twice about it when it's time for the kids to go on the trips. Every parent will pay without a fuss because they don't their children staying home. Saturday morning was exciting for Gwen, Wanda and Shannon, they made plans to go over and meet the rest of Eddy's siblings. They met outside Wanda's house then walked over when Eddy came out to tell them they could come in. The three girls were shocked to learn there was a baby in the house with Eddy. Wanda couldn't believe what she was seeing the house smelled bad and was filthy. "What kind of parent would leave a baby behind?" Shannon answered speaking from experience, "The kind that doesn't care about nobody but themselves." Sadden by what she was seeing she turned and walked out crying a little. She wiped the tears away before Wanda came up to her, "You're okay Shan?" She looked over at Wanda and said, "Yeah, that's too much for me to look at; I can't go back in there. What do we do Wanda? Do we tell so something can be done with their parents? We can't leave them like this." Wanda looks back at the door and says, "If we tell won't they be taken away from them?" They look at each other with a blank stare not sure what to say to each other. Finally, Shannon says, "It depends on what our parents do about it I suppose. Maybe they will make her parents take care of them." Gwen and Eddy come out with the others. Gwen was proud of the way she changed the baby diaper; she made a fresh one out of a clean pillowcase. It was a surprise to her to find clean linen in the filthy house. Eddy's brother Jake who they nick named red man is nine, would go out and steal food for the family when there were none in the house. All the kids could pass for white; their hair colors were black, brown and blond. Jake was the only red head with green eyes. He and Eddy would rotate weeks going to school. They were the only two their mom registered to go. They had two older siblings who were being raised by their aunt, both teenagers a boy and girl. It was Eddy's turn to go the first week of school; Jake would start the second week while Eddy takes care of the others at home. The younger ones never went to school Eddy and Jake would teach them what they leaned. They were smart kids in a horrible situation about as bad as Shannon's. She thought she'd never see children with parents like hers who hate their kids. When Eddy's parents were home both of them would go to school; Jake would sometimes go with no shoes. But that was his plan so the teacher would send him to lost and found. While there he would take extra's for the other kids; but right now, they all looked a hot mess. Shannon and Wanda walked them across the street to show them to Joyce to see if she knew a way to help them. When they walked in the house, they were surprised to see more adults there hanging out. Shannon was shocked to see her parents there, after Barbara acted up so bad at the mall, she just knew Joyce would have nothing else to do with her. She thought who would want to be around a crazy person anyway? Wanda called her mom over to explain what they discovered across the street. Joyce shuffles over and ask, "What is it sweetie?" Wanda looks at Shannon then back at her mom before speaking. "Mom we have a situation that we're going to need your help with." Joyce realizes it's something very serious by the look on both girls' faces. "Hum, hold that thought I'll be right back." She went over to let her company know she has to handle something with the kids. She leads her guest into the entertainment room with the wet bar and closed the door. She came back and sat the girls on the sofa in the living room. "So, what seems to be the problem? She just knew it would be something simple to solve with a few kind words and send them on their way. Wanda motioned to Shannon to tell the story after all she didn't want to get in trouble for tending to other people business, plus the fact that she really didn't know how to explain the situation. Shannon started out telling Joyce how she met Eddy Gal as Wanda went to open the door and let them in. Joyce was appalled at the sight and smell of the dirty children filling her living room; she stopped Shannon from talking in the middle of the story. No kind words are going to make this disappear she thought; then said, "Girls what have you gotten me into?" Looking at how dirty the baby was brought tears to her eyes she was speechless. Joyce remembered seeing a moving truck pull up to the house just before summer. She had every intention of meeting the new neighbors but just never found the time to do so. She wished she would have done so now; she could tell Wanda and Shannon was hurt by what they discovered. "Look girls I can tell this is a bit much for you to handle, it is for me too. One thing I can assure on is that their parents haven't been gone too long. It looks like they're just not properly caring for their children." Reluctantly she asked the children to take her to the house to get them something descent to put on. Gwen took her to the one place that had clean clothes; Eddy helped pick out each child an outfit. Joyce took them all back to her house to clean them up. She put her kids to work with bathing the three little ones in the bathroom and putting the rest outside in the pool to deep clean the dirt out as they swim. Wanda, Shannon and Gwen ironed the clothes. David made sure no one miss behaved and all went well. Joyce came from the garage with a box of clothes she was going to get rid of and told Eddy it was for them to take home with them. She pulled Wanda, Shannon and Gwen aside to say, "To ease ya'll troubled minds I am going to look into the situation and talk to Eddy's parents. I can't promise you the situation will get better but it's a start." The girls face lit up with relief knowing that their new friend was not going to suffer any longer. Joyce really didn't like getting involved in other people's business, but this one needed some intervention. She asked Eddy what her parents' name was, when Eddy told her Joyce heart nearly stopped beating and she almost choked on her own spit as she attempted to swallow. She quickly pulled herself together so the girls wouldn't notice her reaction. "OH, hell no, she thinks to herself as thoughts of panic enter her mind. "I can't mess with this it would ruin it for me." The girls stood silent waiting for Joyce to tell them what to do next. But Joyce mind was in a state of panic, "If I do this it would have to be done in a way no one would find out about me." She nervously smiled at Eddy then told the girls to take them back home because she had something very important to take care of. Wanda thought it was odd the way her mom rushed them out. She ignored it thinking maybe she was in a hurry to talk to the other adults. Eddy's dad name Jerome struck a nerve in Joyce. They were lovers and no one knew it, Joyce was going to make sure no one finds out. Yep, when her husband Greg wasn't around, she got around without him. Eddy's dad wasn't the kind of man you want to rub the wrong way, he has a dangerous temper. Eddy's mom found out the hard way twice; he beat her so bad she nearly died in the hospital both times. But she wouldn't leave him, she claimed she love him too much. Joyce wasn't worried about his temper; she was more worried about her family finding out about her affairs. Oh yes, she's had more than this one. She loves her family but at the same time she loves being the other woman outside the family. She was not about to let anything jeopardize that. She went back to the adults to entertain them as she decided to deal with this later. She noticed all the men had left it was just the ladies. She had invited Claire to join them when she saw her walking home from the graveyard. Reluctantly Claire came in she didn't want to be rude to Joyce. Her eyes were red and puffy from crying so long. It has only been three weeks since Tate's death; he was her only child. She sat quietly listening to the other women chatter wishing she had gone home. As Joyce came in, they all chimed in at the same time, "What took you so long?" She told them about the family across the street. It was better gossip than the stuff they were talking about; it got Claire's attention. Joyce was hoping someone else would be nosey enough to want to look into it besides her. They all were saying how horrible it was for parents to have kids and not care for them. Of course, everybody made a comment about it except

Barbara and Claire. If Barbara were going to say something Joyce was ready to set her free about what she does to her own kids; but Barb didn't utter a word. Linda who is the neighborhood gossiper asks, "When the parents are due back home? "Joyce replies, "Not sure maybe this weekend; you volunteering to go over and get them straight?" Linda quickly responds, "Oh hell no I don't know them like that." They laughed to see Linda back away from finding out the latest gossip. Joyce knows the parents are coming the weekend; it's her time with Romeo as she calls him. Claire spoke for the first time since she's been there. Crying she said, "I was one of those parents; I didn't care what happened to my child now he's gone. If I had just one more chance to be with him, I'd be a better mother." She started crying profusely as no one said a word for about a minute. Finally, Joyce and Linda went over to her to console her then they began crying. Claire began blaming herself for Tate's death. Linda tried giving her words of comfort by telling her she was going to get through it. But Claire went on saying, "I cared more about my drugs than I did my own child, I can't even tell you anything about him or what his favorite food was. I was a horrible mother and now I have no child, I have nothing." Joyce held Claire's hand and said, "You have your husband and you have your life. Don't give up your will to live. Honor your son's life by living yours better. You haven't needed the drugs since his death, don't give up now. You're stronger than you think Claire dig deep within you grab that strength and live." All the ladies gathered around Claire assured her she was going to be okay. The support the ladies showed Claire gave her the courage to freely express the pain and grief she held inside. At the end of it all they managed to get Claire to smile.

It was dark outside as the ladies started leaving to go home. It was a great session with Claire getting her to release all that guilt and blame. They all promised to help her with the grief of losing a child. Joyce walked them outside as they left; she was standing in the driveway alone looking at the house across the street. Romeo was back the lights were on in the house. He'd called her that morning telling her he was on his way back home. He told her to arrange a place for them to meet. They were to meet later that night at a hotel. The thought of being with a man who cared nothing for his children bothered her. He paid her well for the pleasure she gave him, but he wasn't like that with other ladies, Joyce was special to him. He was good to the other ladies as long as he had them on their back, but he was mean as a viper to them. They never knew when he was going to strike them; his wife knew that side of him all too well until she inherited her parents millions. They died in a plane crash on their way home from one of their many vacations they seemed to stay on. Katherine was their only child raised by nannies and housekeepers. Her parents gave her the best of things, just never gave her the best of their time. They were always traveling trying to keep the money flowing drumming up new clients for business. Kate hardly saw either of them; she was in I.C.U for the second time clinging to life herself when she heard about her parents' death. Inheriting the money literally saved her life. Jerome hadn't laid a hand on her since. She always said she'd never leave him because she loved him. He was the first man in her life to give her love and attention she craved for from her parents down to the beatings. She felt like it was what she needed to be loved. The children were just the residue of trying to fulfill the desire of wanting to be loved. She was being to her kids what her mom was to her, never there. Kate and Romeo were busy traveling and spending money on lavish hotels and dinning at expensive restaurants. She wouldn't buy fancy jewelry or clothes for herself or the kids. She felt getting all that as a kid got her nothing. She wasn't foolish with her inheritance; she made some smart investments in the stock market and set aside each child a sizeable trust fund to inherit when they turn eighteen. She figured it's something to start their adult lives with. If they want more, they'll have to earn it or wait for her to die and get what's left if any, just like her parents did her. Kate's sense of mothering is way off from her parents. They made sure her living was good; to her it was nothing. She's giving her children nothing to live for, but she thinks it's good for them. Funny how life put us on a merry go round spinning going nowhere. Most of us are not smart enough to get off when it slows down. Instead we lead our children to the same merry go round to go nowhere and think it's the right thing to do.

Kate knew Jerome had other women she didn't care. He needs her now and she is going to lead him around like a puppet on a string. One wrong move from him and she is cutting him off. Having her inheritance has giving her the strength she needs to get away from Romeo; so why hasn't she left? Kate has asked herself that question over and over; only to discover she likes controlling the man who controlled her with fear. She feels it's her turn to have the power of control in her hands. Romeo doesn't like being controlled by a woman, that's why he's been taking out his anger on the other women. He's getting more and more out of control. He's at the threshold of becoming a killer; it's getting harder for him to control his anger. Joyce is the only woman he hasn't had to hit. Perhaps it's because he knows they both are living double lives. Or it could be Joyce doesn't demand anything of him because her husband gives her everything but his time. Jerome's only required to give her pleasure; the thought of that made him feel he was at least in control of something. Romeo goes over to the living room window, he sees Joyce standing in her driveway. He gives the signal that he's ready to meet her and walks away from the window. Joyce walks back in the house before Kate gets to the window to see who or what Romeo was looking at. She only saw Claire walking on her way back home. Kate knows Claire goes to the graveyard to visit the resting place of her son. She knows what's left of Claire is nothing her husband desires; she walks away from the window. Every time they come home, he goes and looks out the window as if he's looking for someone and then he leaves.

Claire makes it to her street, as she turns the corner to head home, she stops in front of a church on the corner. She is surprised to see it open on Saturday night. The parking lot is full of cars and there is a live performance of music playing inside. All the years she's lived here she never knew a church was on this corner not far from her house. The name on the sign read: PENTECOSTAL CHURCH OF DELIVERANCE. After reading the sign Claire said out loud, "I need deliverance." She turned and walked in the church and headed straight at the altar and kneeled down. The group singing finished their performance and left the front as the pastor approached Claire. Everyone there knew of Claire except a few visitors from out of town. Claire was the addict that would stumble across the church lawn trying to get home, only to end up passed out at the entrance of the door. The pastor and deacons would discover her every Sunday morning. They would pray for her and take home to her son. Claire never remembered how she got home; she would wake up wishing she wasn't there needing another high. A few ladies joined the pastor at the altar as he asks, "What is your name?" She told him, "Claire." "Look at me Mrs. Claire." She looked up with tears rolling from her eyes. The pastor asked her, "What do you want and need Jesus to do for you?" Claire simply said, "I need deliverance, I want to be free from this pain I have inside. Can Jesus do that?" The women standing around her began crying with her. The pastor was filled with compassion and excitement to finally see Claire come in the church seeking God than passing out from being high outside the door. He gets the microphone and announces to the congregation that God has changed the order of the program. The congregation responded with a heartfelt AMEN. Everyone stood and held hands to help support Claire in seeking deliverance. Claire desperately wanted to be free from the heaviness in her heart, she said whatever the pastor told her to say. The last thing she remember saying was the scripture Romans 10:9, 10; then she woke up to them helping her off the floor. She didn't remember passing out just feeling light as a feather flying away. As she stood to her feet she began laughing so much and just started hugging everybody. She felt like a brand-new person filled with so much love and joy. Music began playing as the church celebrated Claire's freedom. She stayed until the singing was over, but everybody told her she was the miracle of the evening. She couldn't wait to get home and tell her husband Daniel that she is a new person. Daniel was still driving trucks; since Tate's death he was taking long hauls that would keep him away from home for weeks. He's doing local runs and is usually home by evening. Like his wife Daniel blamed himself for Tate's death. He couldn't grieve like Claire because he felt that he needed to take care of her.

Always he tells himself he should have been home more being a father and a better husband none of this would've happened. But now that he's home he's going to man up and fix it. He goes over his plan of action in his head: I got to get Claire off the drugs, she deserves better. I'm going to be a real good husband to her she deserves my best. How could I have put that kind of responsibility on my son? A real man wouldn't have done that. After the funeral Daniel was prepared to deal with Claire's drug addiction, but the grief of losing her only child proved to be a strong cure. There were no withdrawals' only weeping and whaling's. He couldn't get her to leave the house the first week; the second week he had to force her to come home from the graveyard. Night and day, she would cry saying she could've been a better mother. This week he didn't have to bring her home, she was coming on her own. But tonight, as these thoughts flow through his mind, he is preparing a special dinner for Claire when she comes home. He bought her new clothes, shoes, purse and perfumes. The house has been cleaned and filled with new furniture; it's going to bring a smile to her face he hopes. It's up to him to bring the romance back in their lives; it's been so long since he's done that. He's feeling a little nervous then smile. He can't believe he's feeling like a teenager trying to win over the girl of his dreams. Just as he finished setting the table Claire comes in beaming with joy saying, "Daniel you won't believe what just happened to me!" "It feels good to have you smiling like that; sit down and tell me all about its babe." He directs her over to the new sofa to sit. "Wow, you got us new furniture it's beautiful!" Excited she turns around and hugs him tight. "So, what's the good news?" They sat down as she began telling him what happened when she walked in the church on the corner. A tear rolled down his cheek as he reached over and gently touched her face with his hand. The skin on her face was dry and flakey from years of drug abuse. To him she was as beautiful as she was when they met. He kisses her as if he was falling in love for the first time. He guided her to the room to show her the outfit he bought her. Since God provided the smile, he thought it only fitting for him to bring the romance. It was the beginning of many new beginnings for the two of them. After a night of love and passion they went to church together Sunday morning. Daniel gave his life to Jesus and they both joined the church, after service they walked to the graveyard. Daniel apologized to his son and promised he would be a man and take care of Claire.

Monday began the second week of school. They all noticed that Darren still was not in school, they were only told that he was still sick in the hospital. Darren couldn't deal with the loss of his friend who was more like his brother. His parents had to admit him in a mental institution to help him deal with the loss. David was the main leader of the gang now he made sure he was on the visitor's list to go see Darren. The first visit was hard for him to bear seeing his friend so disoriented made him cry like never before.

He decided to wait a while to visit when he is strong enough handle what he sees.

For Shannon it was always a rough start of a week. She had to bathe and dress Sasha to get her out the house on time to catch the bus. Kindergartners' and first graders' catch the bus because of the busy highway they had to cross to get to the school. James didn't want to go back because he knew he would be tortured to use his right hand, plus the fact that he still couldn't read or understand what was being taught. Shannon made him take his soiled linen off the bed so they could set the mattress outside to dry. They left the house early to eat breakfast at Joyce. She loved cooking a big breakfast for the kids. They finished eating and started out for school, they were surprised to see Eddy with her other siblings coming to school together. They all were clean with new clothes and shoes. The group gathered in the middle of the street to compliment Eddy on how nice they looked. Somehow, they managed to make it to school on time. Shannon went to check on Sasha making sure she was alright in class. Eddy looked in the class at her sister Rebecca who was sitting on the other side with white kids. She didn't pay any attention to the set up in the class. "Your little sister is so cute and too tiny for first grade." Shannon smiled and said, "Yep, but she's too smart for first grade she doesn't know it yet. By next week I'll be hearing about it." Wanda said to Eddy, "That little girl knows how to read better than me and knows her multiplications up to fifteen! I can barely get through the twelves. You are teaching her way too much Shannon." They laughed as they walked to their classes. Shannon felt something wasn't right with her teacher when she walked in the classroom. She was beginning to think Miss Belinda didn't like her. But she didn't want to believe that, she is just a child. What did she do to make an adult hate her? The last bell rang, and Miss Belinda called the class to order. She started out giving the class a quiz to take. The whole class let out AWE at the thought of having to use their brain on the second week of school. Miss Belinda had a busy itinerary planned for the morning and learning games for the afternoon to give their brains a break after lunch.

James got in his class and ran to the back hoping the teacher wouldn't notice him today. He doesn't understand why she won't let him use his left hand. He tries his best to learn but he just can't remember what he learned. As he took a seat, he thought to himself, "I hope she doesn't bother me today I'm going home if she does." But it turned out to be his lucky day, Jake was in class with him and he was more trouble than the teacher could handle. The first two hours of class was spent getting Jake under control. Finally, she was able to get to James to see if he was participating with the class assignments. It was no surprise to her to see nothing written on his paper she asked him, "James do you intend to do any work in class today?" He just looked at her too afraid to say anything.

She started going over some of the work with him a few times only to get nothing accomplished. Before she could scold him about its Jake was up disrupting the class again. It took forty-five minutes to get him calmed down to do his lesson. She realized she was going to have to go step by step with James. But before she could pull up a chair to sit beside him, he jumped up and ran out of the class with Jake behind him.

Sasha knew her day was not going to be good the moment her teacher separated the class with blacks on one side and whites on the other. Mrs. Vinegar explained she was putting the slower learners on one side because she didn't want them slowing down her fast learners. But Sasha knew it was because she didn't like her black students. There were ten blacks and eleven whites in the class, but she seated nine blacks at the table she moved to the corner. She put Rebecca on the side with the white kids. Rebecca didn't like Sasha at all because everybody always called Sasha cute little girl. She felt that she was just as cute, but nobody ever tells her she is except her mom. Mrs. Vinegar gave everybody the reading book Dick and Jane to practice reading. Sasha looked at the book and thought to herself, "I already know how to read this book it's too easy." Instead of complaining about it she read the entire book while Mrs. Vinegar went over the first three pages with the other students. She intended not to go over the lesson with the black kids. After twenty minutes Sasha knew they were on their own for learning. The other children just started talking about their favorite thing to do during play time. Sasha asked them, "Aren't you guys going to read the book?" No one answered her they looked at her then turned away and kept talking. Sasha completed the worksheet then got up and put it on the teacher's desk. She looked out the window and saw James and Jake run out of their class. She quickly walks over to the door to catch them passing by. She stands in the door and yells, "James where are you going?" The boys didn't stop they just kept running. Mrs. Vinegar turned to see Sasha yelling out the door; angrily she asked, "Little girl what are you doing out of your seat? Get over there and do your work right now!" The others laugh as Sasha runs back to her seat but stops when Sasha answered. "I've already finished my work that book is too easy for me. You would have known that if you were over here teaching us. And that was my brother running away from school." The class got quiet because they knew Sasha was in big trouble for telling the teacher what she was doing was wrong. Mrs. Vinegar was furious at the fact that the smallest student in class is causing her problems. "Sit down in your seat right now Sasha or I will send you to the office," she said with a stern look on her face. But that did not scare Sasha one bit she yells back, "Well send me there and I will tell how you are not teaching us black kids." Sasha sat down in her chair folded her arms with a mean frown on her face and her bottom lip poked out. The whole class said, "Oooh," surprised at Sasha's defiance towards the teacher.

Mrs. Vinegar felt like she just wanted to take Sasha and throw her out of the class; but she knew she would be in some serious trouble with the principle if he knew she was separating the class by color. She told the class to settle down then asked Sasha, "Where is your work? Sasha still frowning said, "On your desk." Mrs. Vinegar walked over to her desk picked up the worksheet and looked it over. To her surprise it was done correctly. She looked over at Sasha and saw that she was still pouting. She went over to Sasha and asked her to read the first six pages in the book. Sasha quickly read the pages without stumbling over one word. Mrs. Vinegar told her to read a few more hoping she would make a mistake, but Sasha read the whole book in no time proving to the teacher she could read. Mrs. Vinegar was beside herself with Sasha, she wasn't used to dealing with a child as smart as Sasha. She told the other side to do the worksheet. She then pulled a chair over to the table and began working with the black students. As she was going over the words with them Sasha couldn't help but notice that the others couldn't read that well. Butch was big for his age he always bullied the others to do what he says to do. When it was his turn to read, he stumbled over sounding out the vowels, Sasha got impatient and said the word for him. Mrs. Vinegar told her to calm down and give the others a chance to learn. Sasha thought all the kids could read like her she just said, "But they should know this already; what's wrong with them?" Mrs. Vinegar smiled as she realized Sasha thought everybody could read like her. Mrs. Vinegar let Sasha help with pronouncing the words correctly; Larry and Pam were pretty good at reading. The teacher noticed Sasha would spell the word before pronouncing it; she did it out of habit not knowing the others couldn't spell that well. Mrs. Vinegar mumbled to herself, "She is too smart for her own good." She looked up at the clock and saw it was almost time for lunch. "Okay class time to line up and wash our hands for lunch." The children were happy it was lunch time they lined up and followed the teacher down the hall to the bathrooms to wash up. As they got in the cafeteria Mrs. Vinegar realized she had to help Sasha with getting her lunch because she was too short to see over the tray rail. She carried the tray for Sasha to the table then noticed the table was too high for her to sit and eat. At first sight of Sasha Mrs. Vinegar was sure she was too young for the class; but after her performance in class Mrs. Vinegar is convinced that Sasha needs to be in a higher grade like third or fourth. She went and found a thick book for Sasha to sit on although Sasha was used to standing in the chair to eat, Mrs. Vinegar wasn't having it. Mrs. Vinegar may have her issues with color; but a smart child is a smart child. She made a mental note to go talk with the principle about Sasha's learning abilities. After lunch they have one hour left in class then are dismissed early to catch the bus home. Sasha couldn't wait to get home and wait for Shannon to tell how her day started out so bad. She couldn't believe she was in class with kids that couldn't read or spell like she could. I wonder if they know their numbers she thought; they are not normal if they don't. They went back to class; as the teacher is helping everyone else finish the worksheet together, one little girl interrupts to ask if she could go to the bathroom. Mrs. Vinegar is upset with the idea that she is being interrupted angrily said "No!" The girl's name is Susan she sat in her chair looking scared and confused at why she is not allowed to go. Sasha is surprised Mrs. Vinegar would not let the girl go she is white. Susan waited five minutes and asked again; "Mrs. Vinegar please, I really have to go." She started crying as she cupped her hands between her thighs and pressed them together bouncing up and down. Mrs. Vinegar yelled at Susan, "No!" Susan jumped startled by the yell and lost control; there was a steady stream of fluid flowing down her legs. She stood there crying in a puddle of piss. The students are shocked at what just happened; how could she not let Susan go? Then it got worse, Mrs. Vinegar was angry she wet the floor then made poor little Susan clean it up with paper towels. Susan felt so ashamed everybody saw her wet in her clothes. She had to sit out the rest of the remaining minutes in class with wet clothes on. Mrs. Vinegar made it perfectly clear that there is only one-bathroom break. All the children were afraid of the thought having only one-bathroom break. Sasha made up her mind that she was not going to pee on herself. She didn't know what she was going to do if she had to go and couldn't. The bell rang and class was over for them they were more than ready to leave after that incident. They were all shocked at how mean Mrs. Vinegar acted with Susan; poor Susan she was still crying feeling humiliated for wetting herself in front of the class. As the buses pulled in to pick up the children it was lunch break for the older ones. Shannon hurried down the stairs to catch up with Sasha before she gets on the bus. Sasha stood at back of the line facing the school hoping to get a glimpse of Shannon going to lunch. She sees her sister jumping downstairs then run towards her. They only had about two minutes or less before Sasha gets on the bus. Shannon asked winded, "Are you okay? Do you need anything? Sasha pressed for time replied, "No, James and Jake ran away they're not at school. As Shannon lifts Sasha up on the first step she tells her, "I'll look into it." The driver helps Sasha up the rest of the way waits for her to take a seat and pulls away. Shannon runs back to Gwen, Wanda and Eddy and tells them Jake and James ran away from school this morning. They got her lunch and saved a seat for her at their table. "Why would they run away from school?" The three of them sounded like they were singing in a choir. They all yelled, Jinx! Jinx again! Jinx infinity! Eddy yelled to break the three-way tie. They even laughed at the same time, Shannon shook her head side to side and said, "Okay choir. I have an idea why James would run away; he's a slow learner he doesn't remember what you teach him." "Wow!" The three chimed together again then burst out laughing. Eddy said, "Jake is just bad he won't sit down long enough to learn anything. I can see why he ran home; he probably drove the teacher crazy." They finished eating had a little time for some girl talk then went back to class.

As promised Miss. Belinda did not give them class work since they worked all morning. She let them mingle together a bit while she prepared the games. She noticed all the boys gathered around Shannon and Eddy who wasn't particularly interested in talking to the boys. A surge of jealousy rose up in Belinda; usually she'd be chasing the giggly wide-eyed boys away from her desk. This year the moment that tall light skinned heifer walked through her door; all heads turned to her as if no one else were in the room. And when she smiles it's as if all the boys are put under her spell. Belinda tried to shake off the horrible thoughts she was having about Shannon. They quickly came back the moment she saw Shannon smile. "Huh, looks like I'm going to have to teach you a lesson little girl," she mumbles just before she calls the class to order. "We are going to playboys against girls with multiple choice questions should be fun let's see what you know. Whoever answers a question wrong the other team gets to challenge them with a dare and you have to do it; so, let's not get crazy with dares." Belinda knows Shannon would get all the questions right she's just that smart, but she put together a trick question just for Shannon. She only needed one of the boys to carry out the dare she came up with for Shannon that she knows she won't do. She called Devin over because she knew he has a major crush on Shannon who won't give him a glance. She asked him if he would do anything to get Shannon to like him; he didn't hesitate to say yes. She gave him the question she would be asking Shannon then told him what to dare her to do. Devin wanted no parts of it when he heard what it was and said, "But she won't let me do that; isn't it wrong if she doesn't want to do that? Belinda reminded him the rule of the game you have to do what is dared. Then she said, "Don't worry about her doing it, I'll make her." He agreed then went and stood with the other boys. They were enjoying the game until the girls started winning. They were up fifteen points over the boys. The boys were getting frustrated because the girls had them barking, jumping, making animal sounds and tricks. Once the boys started complaining the dares were unfair Belinda signaled to Devin, she is going to ask the question. She knew by this time Devin wasn't thinking about right or wrong he just wanted the boys to get a chance to dare the girls for a change and win a point. Belinda asked Shannon the question she answered it right, but Belinda told her it was wrong. Shannon and the girls were shocked. Belinda worded it where you had to give a two-part answer, Shannon only gave one. Shannon moved to the middle of the class to except the dare challenge. Devin steps forward excited but nervous because his moral compass inside was tell him this is wrong don't do it. When she saw Devin stepping towards her, she let out a sigh and shook her head.

Devin got mad because he figured Shannon didn't want to be bothered with him; so, he boldly stepped close to her and said, "I dare you to kiss me." Shannon with a look of disgust on her face said, "Ewe no way I'm not kissing you that is just nasty." A normal response for ten years old, the girls giggled and said ewe as the boys cheered Devin on to do it. Miss Belinda stood up and said to Shannon, "Follow the rule everybody else did theirs. You think you're special or something?" Shannon with her arms folded said to Belinda, "I'm not kissing a boy and you can't make me!" The class was shocked that the teacher was allowing the kiss to happen. Belinda stepped up to Shannon and grabbed her before Shannon could react to pull away from her. Belinda slammed Shannon down on one of the desks and held her there then told Devin to kiss her. Shannon started kicking and screaming no, no, no, let me go!" Devin ran over carefully avoiding flailing legs grabbed Shannon's face and landed a juicy kiss on her lips. Shannon hocked up a thick wad of thick snot and spit in his face. Tears are flowing down her face like a river. The boys are laughing at Devin as the spit lands over his left eye with a tail dangling like a rubber band. The girls were standing in silence with both hands covering their mouth not believing what just happened. How could a teacher do this to a student? Some of them started crying saying, "Oh no." Shannon broke free from Belinda and ran through the door yelling, "I'm going to tell my mom!" She disappeared as she ran down the stairs. Eddy grabbed Shannon's things and walked out she told Wanda what happened then went to the office to report it the principle and headed home. Wanda went to every gang member class to let them know about it. It was upsetting to everyone how a teacher could humiliate a student in front of the class like that. Belinda was smiling ear to ear at what she'd done and acted like she didn't have a care in the world. When the principle called over the intercom for her to come to his office that smile vanished. All of a sudden, she realized there will be consequences for her actions. The class sat quiet while Belinda was gone. Devin was more nervous now than he was before it all happened. He wished he'd never listened to the teacher. Wanda came in the class angry as ever and asked, "Who's the boy?" The whole class pointed at Devin without hesitation. Wanda let Devin know who Shannon had then warned him to watch his back because her gang now knows who he is. She turned and walked out the door. Devin knew he was in some serious trouble now his gut was telling him it was wrong. He's got to figure out a way to get home without getting beat up. All of a sudden, he jumped up and ran out the classroom.

Shannon made it home in no time she's a very fast runner. She told Barbara everything that happened in the class. Normally she wouldn't want her mom involved in things because Barb would just embarrass her. This situation needs a big dose of some Barbara embarrassment. Barb flipped out at what she just heard concerning her child. She wasn't good at loving her kids but didn't like other people harming her kids. She adds a whole new meaning to angry mama. She told Shannon she will take care of it first thing in the morning. Shannon went in the room and told Sasha and James what happened to her in school. James told her why he and Jake ran away; Shannon softly spoke to James saying, "You can't go through life not knowing anything James please try harder to learn don't give up." The three of them were hugging when Eddy knocked on the door of their room that was off the patio. Eddy handed Shannon her purse and books then asked, "Are you okay?" Shannon answered, "I'm fine now that mom is going to take care of it in the morning. She gets crazy out of control when someone mess with her kids. Miss Belinda is going to wish she never met my mom." Wanda came up along with the rest of the gang including the teenagers. They assured Shannon they were going to take care of Belinda. Shannon said, "No guys I don't want any of you to get in trouble. My mom will take care of it in a way you won't believe, trust me my mom is punishment enough for Belinda." They agreed with Shannon to let her mom handle it; but as they were walking back to Wanda's house, they agreed to get somebody else to handle it for them. Nobody messes with one of them and get away with it.

The next morning Shannon got everyone ready for school as usual even James. She didn't walk to school with the others because she didn't want to miss the action with her mom. She knows the principle is not going to be able to handle her mom. They set out walking to school Barbara was already madder than a hornets' nest. She was walking faster than a runner; Shannon was doing just that to keep up. She didn't complain about it because she couldn't wait to get to school. They got there faster than Shannon expected the last bell did not ring yet. The children were making their way to classes before the last bell rings. Shannon and Barb pass by Sasha's class going to the office she waved at Sasha while running behind Barb. They walked in the office and Barb asked if she could talk to principle Bailey concerning what happened to her daughter in class yesterday. Barb spoke soft and acted very polite with the secretary. Shannon looked her over to see if she was still her mom, she never heard her talk like that before. Mr. Bailey invited them into his office thinking it was going to be a simple discussion and handling a misunderstanding based off the information Belinda gave him. When Shannon told her side of the story which coincided with Eddy's he realized Belinda lied to him. He decided to call Belinda in the office to straighten it out with the parent being present. He didn't know it yet, but he will be regretting he made that decision later. Barbara was being so calm and polite acting like she wouldn't hurt a fly; the fact that she was pregnant you wouldn't think she would. Shannon knew the act wasn't going to last long somebody is going to pull the trigger that will set her off. Belinda walked in Mr. Bailey's office and Barbs temper lid hit the ceiling. She popped up out of her chair and yelled, "You put your hands on my child! Nobody puts their hands on mine but me!" Before anybody could react, Barb grabbed Belinda by her hair and started hitting her on the head, face, and back wherever her fist landed. Belinda started screaming and pull away to try and run. Mr. Bailey fell on the floor when He pushed away from the desk off balanced. He got up yelling, "Mrs. Kingsley please!" Before he got close enough to break them apart, Belinda somehow managed to slip away and bolted out the door of his office. Barb was tight on her tail hitting the back of her head. The people in the front office moved out the way as Belinda trips over a chair and rolls towards the door. As usual she had on a cute short dress that gave a clear view of her cute pink panties and half of a butt cheek. There was no dignity to be lost when you are running for your life. Belinda popped up off the floor before Barb could get a lick in while she was down and ran out the door down the hall screaming. Mr. Bailey came running out behind them still yelling, "Mrs. Kingsley please stop this!" Shannon is right behind him laughing hysterically. Belinda turns the corner and heads for the parking lot to her car. Barb is not far behind she turns the corner and throws her heavy purse at Belinda. Surprisingly the purse hit Belinda in the back and knocks her off balance; she stumbled and rolled again. Shannon is leaning against the wall laughing too hard to stand up. Mr. Bailey finally makes it around the corner still yelling, "Stop this, Stop this now! Belinda gets up once again before Barb gets to her and makes it to her car to speed off home. Mr. Bailey was still yelling at Barb until she picked up her purse turned to him with a look that said you're next. He literally slid to a stop in the grass turned around and ran back to the office. Barb didn't run after him though; she walked over to Shannon and said, "You go to class now she won't be bothering you again." Shannon skipped down the hall and ran up the stairs with a smile on her face. Barb headed home satisfied with the results of her parent teacher conference. Sasha's class heard all the noise but couldn't see what was going on because Mrs. Vinegar always closes the door once the last bell rings. Sasha knew it involved her mom and Shannon's teacher she'll find out when she gets home. Mr. Bailey got his office back in order then sent one of the ladies in the office to teach Belinda's class for the day. He had the secretary call the school board for a sub for Belinda's class tomorrow. He was leaving to meet with the superintendent about the whole matter. At the end of it all Devin was suspended for two weeks after he told his side of things. Miss Belinda was suspended for a month. Shannon was happy her mom's craziness came to her rescue when she needed it to. By Saturday everyone who heard the rumor was at Joyce house to get more details even the adults. Shannon reenacted the whole thing; they all were in tears from laughing so hard even Barbara. The boys were calling Belinda by the nick name they call her at school: Ms. Pussy lips. When the adults figured out who they were calling pussy lips they told them to stop. "It's not nice to call adults' names that are disrespectful. All the kids let out a loud sigh because they knew a long speech about what is right, what is wrong and good behavior was coming. They were looking at Joyce to stand and start but Linda stood up. "I just want to say that I am so proud of the way you guys changed and is not gang battling with each other anymore. You are cleaning up the neighborhoods rather than destroying them. Calling people negative names because they are different is bullying; don't pick up the bad habits stay a positive community. The little ones looking and learning from you they repeat everything. Let's keep the future of the community positive okay." They all replied, "Okay Mrs. Linda." Sasha heard the boys call Miss Belinda pussy lips she thought to herself, "That's an odd name to have," she stepped out and went to the bathroom when Joyce was telling them not to say that name again. Shannon never told Sasha her teacher's name; Sasha figured pussy lips was it. Belinda always passed by Sasha's class in the mornings coming from the office. Sasha never spoke to her because she never knew her name, but now she knows and will for sure speak to her the next time she sees her. Since everybody was talking about how Barbara went to the school and caused much chaos, Sasha didn't get a chance to tell how her teacher has the kids wetting their clothes by not allowing a bathroom break after lunch. Six kids had wet their clothes by the end of the week. Sasha thought by now somebody's parents would be at the school trying to find out what was going on. She found out Friday on the bus ride home the children were more afraid of getting in trouble with their parents for having wet clothes. They were not telling their parents why their clothes were wet. It was making Sasha nervous she knows one day it's going to happen to her. Since her mom came to Shannon's rescue, she now knows it's safe to go to her mom if it happens to her.

Shannon was proud that Barbara came to defend her when she needed her to, she felt safe at school. She knew no one else would do anything to her they will experience nightmare Barbara. Although she was surprised to learn they wasn't removing her out of the class; it felt awkward walking in class smiling at a teacher you know hates you. Miss. Belinda couldn't look Shannon in the face since the incident happened; Shannon managed to control not laughing at her as time passed. Devin apologized when he came back; Shannon accepted the apology but told him to stay out of her face. The boys wouldn't let him forget the fatal kiss they called it. There was less stress for Shannon since her teacher was not out to get her. She didn't know Belinda disliked her that much and she couldn't understand why an adult have that much hatred for a child.

Sasha's situation had gotten worse more and more kids had wet their clothes. Sasha couldn't believe they were not telling their parents. So far, she is lucky she hasn't had to go after lunch, but she knows her time is coming, and she is ready to handle it. Mrs. Vinegar is mean to all the kids not just the blacks. Rebecca still did not like Sasha until Mrs. Vinegar put her on the side with Sasha for not reading like she should. Sasha was helping everyone at her table with their reading, but she was having issues with writing. She was writing her letter "S" backwards and her "M" upside down. Mrs. Vinegar noticed that she was writing correctly with the practice sheet following the dotted lines. After going back and forth with Sasha correcting the same letters, she had Sasha tested to see if there were a problem with her identifying certain letters. The test results came back determining that Sash was slightly dyslexic. Since Sasha's learning ability was so far ahead of the class, they arranged for her to go to a learning center to learn how to overcome her dyslexia. Mrs. Vinegar didn't like that at all; it meant she had to teach the black kids herself. But it wasn't as bad as she thought somehow in a month's time Sasha had the children reading better than the ones she was teaching. They would not say how Sasha had them reading so well; it just gave her one more reason not to like Sasha. Mrs. Vinegar wasn't all that bad she did talk to the principle about having Sasha possibly moved up two grades. After seeing Sasha with the other first graders and how tiny she looked with them; Mr. Bailey told Mrs. Vinegar he'd be concerned moving a tiny girl in a class with children that towered over her he feels they will take advantage of her. But he did say he will talk with Sasha's parents to see if they would consider it. When he found out Barbara Kingsley was Sasha's mom his heart skipped a beat. He really did not want to deal with Barb again but considering this is something positive he hopes the outcome will be better. The meeting with Barbara went smoother than expected she feared the same thing as Mr. Bailey that Sasha was too small. Mrs. Vinegar couldn't make the meeting, but the principle let her know the grade change will not take place. When Sasha found out she was surprised that Mrs. Vinegar wanted to advance her up she figured Mrs. Vinegar was just mean.

Daniel went back to work since Claire was doing well off the drugs so far. She was still making daily trips to the graveyard but spending less time there. She is keeping herself busy by going to noon day prayer at the church to learn more about the bible and her faith in God. When it was over, she would stay late to clean the church so the mothers wouldn't have to do it. The mothers loved having Claire with them because she was so eager to learn from them; they were just as eager to teach her. Claire started bringing sandwiches and drinks for them to have to eat. She noticed during prayer stomachs were growling loud, but no one complained of being hungry. She wouldn't ask them if they needed something to eat, she just decided to bring the food. She knows there's not much you can get on a fixed income it's only fair to help those who help you she thought. Their teachings were simple but what really stirred Claire's soul was learning about God's unconditional love. How powerful it is and how it covered a multitude of sin. It's like her spirit woke up and leaped for joy. For the first time she understood that God loved her enough to cover all the wrong she had done. The next day she got up early to go to the graveyard. She decided to take a different way to get there. She took the dirt path behind the houses on Shannon's street. As she was passing by Eddy's house, she noticed the back door was open and inside looked dark. She stopped to take a look to see if the house was empty and in good condition; but then she remembered it was the house across from Joyce where the children were being neglected. She knocked on the open door before stepping in to see if the children were there. "Hello, is anybody home?" No one answered at first. "I'm not here to hurt you I just want to know if you're okay." Two teenagers came forward out of the dark a boy and girl holding a baby. The boy spoke up, "Yes Mrs. Claire we're okay." She was surprised he knew her name, so she asked, "What are your names?" "Well, my name is Kenny, and this is my sister Stacey with baby Queen and two-year-old Shawanda and three-year-old Benjamin." Claire stepped in to get a closer look at the baby she forgot she was going to the graveyard. She looks around and said, "Let me guess, no lights?" They both repeated, "No lights." Claire just shook her head and asked, "Are you guys hungry?" They both shook their heads and said, "Yes." She told them to come with her to her house and she will feed them. There was only the five of them, so Claire asked, "Where are the others?" Stacey finally decided to talk, "They're in school, and mom brought us here to keep the babies so the others could go to school. We were living just fine with our auntie. She did register us in school, but we have to stay home to keep the babies. Eddy and Red man told us to take turns like they use to do." Claire fed the children then went and paid their utility bills so they could have water and lights. She began teaching them how to take care of themselves better. She cooked dinner for them at their house and told them not to let anyone know she was helping them. They all agreed to keep it a secret they didn't want Claire to stop coming over. She made sure they kept the lights out at night she told them it would draw attention to them if people knew they were home alone all the time. She mainly didn't want Joyce thinking their dad was back; she figured out Joyce and Romeo had a thing going and didn't want it to interfere with the love she has for the children. She has to figure out a way to get them without it causing a big mess. All the big kids were going to school as Claire was keeping the three little ones with her. The church mothers enjoyed the kids; Claire told them she was babysitting so no one questioned who the parents were. As a junky Claire had a run in with Romeo, she knows he's mean and dangerous. She couldn't stand by and let the children suffer as she was so wrapped up with taking care of them; she had not noticed she hadn't been to the graveyard. Claire told her husband about the children and their parents. At first, he didn't want her involved because he knew about their father and how bad he treated women. He saw the joy the children bought in her life, so he didn't push the issue. At least she wasn't spending so much time in the graveyard the children gave her purpose. He was going to make sure no harm was going to come to his wife. They went shopping and got some food for them but not too much that would cause attention from the parents whenever they would come home. Daniel told Claire not to change the situation for the children too much that way they'll be able to get the children legally; it'll all work out in her favor. He couldn't believe he was helping his wife plot to take some else kids. He knew her love for the children came from the loss of her own. He made a promise that he would be a better husband to her, if it means taking children from bad parents so be it. She's not on drugs, not at a grave site and she's smiling that's good enough for him. Saturdays Claire started having bible study in the front yard of the children's house with all the children in the neighborhood. It was getting close to Halloween she wanted them to know the bible stories not candy, witches and demons. The children were happy to spend the time with Claire she was really fun to be with. She made the stories come to life and funny by acting out the scenes. Eddy's parents still had not come home it is the longest they ever stayed away. Joyce saw that the yard was filling up with children from everywhere; so, she told Claire to bring them to her house and she will provide snacks and drinks for them. Claire didn't know the gang decided to make her their gang mother in honor of Tate. Seeing her teaching them made them think of Tate a lot; quite a few teens started going to church with Claire on Sunday's. Since Claire gave her life to Jesus everybody loved the person she'd become. She shared her life story with anyone who asked. Taking care of Kate's children filled a void in her; she found out from the doctor she would never be able to have any more kids because the drugs she was addicted to caused damage. Kate's baby gave her the second chance she needs to prove she can be a better mother than she was with Tate. Daniel was cautious about Claire taking care of Romeo and Kate's kids; he knew Romeo had a dangerous temper; they had a few bouts with Daniel getting the best of Romeo every time. Daniel knows Romeo is a killer waiting to happen and he's prepared to protect his wife from that killer.

Sasha was back in class with the others only to find that Mrs. Vinegar still was not letting them go to the bathroom after lunch. The room was starting to have a strong urine smell. Sasha asked the others why they haven't told their parents to stop it. They said they were more afraid of what the teacher would do to them afterwards. It made Sasha feel very sad to see the teacher not giving them a bathroom break; she never had the chance to mention it to Barbara with all the drama going on with Shannon and her teacher. Since then Barb has found out James Jr. hasn't been going to school for weeks. Sasha felt no one had time for her minor problem and can't understand why the others had not told their parents. She made up her mind that today she was going to tell her mom about it no matter what was going on. As they used the bathroom and washed their hands before lunch, Sasha could see fear in all of her classmates' faces. The worst part was when they got in the cafeteria, they saw apple juice being severed with their lunch. They all sighed, "Oh no." If they drink the apple juice it means going to the bathroom faster than they want; if they drink a little bit, the teacher wants to let them throw away the rest. They all ate quietly worried about what was going to happen to them after lunch. They were in class thirty minutes when three kids started doing the pee- pee dance crying and begging to go to the bathroom. Mrs. Vinegar wouldn't allow it they all wet their clothes. It made the others sad to see it happen again. Ten minutes later Sasha had to go; she planned on holding it until class was over but that would be in forty-five minutes, she couldn't hold it that long. She asked if she could go use the bathroom; of course, the teacher said no, But Sasha was not planning on wetting her clothes, so she waited two minutes before asking again. This time she walked up to Mrs. Vinegar desk and asked if she could go. Angrily Mrs. Vinegar yells, "No, why are you still asking me that when you know I am not going to allow you go?" Sasha stood still for a moment then pulled of her under wear and let go on Mrs. Vinegar foot. Sasha wipes herself with a napkin put on her under wear and ran just as Mrs. Vinegar screamed as the hot liquid runs over her foot down into her shoe. Sasha yells back at her from the door, "I'm telling my mom on you and you're gonna get it!" Mrs. Vinegar stood up and shook the shoe full of pee off her foot and yells at Sasha as she runs out the door, "How dare you nasty little girl!" The others jumped out of their seats and ran out screaming behind Sasha to get on the buses waiting by the curb. Mrs. Vinegar looked around the empty class and mumbled, "I knew that little girl was going to be trouble from the moment she stepped in my class." But Mrs. Vinegar is about to know the wrath of Barbara for not letting her child go to the bathroom. As soon as Sasha got home, she let Barb know what the teacher had been doing to the class. Barb grabbed her purse and Sasha and headed to Joyce to ask her if she could take her to the school to settle a matter before it close. She told Joyce what Sasha had told her which made Joyce upset to hear a teacher would do such a thing. Joyce grabbed her purse, car keys and her baby boy Val who is three and headed to the car. Her main reason for taking Barb is to keep her under control seeing that she is very pregnant now. She knows oh too well how angry Barb gets; but when it comes to her children, she loses her mind. It's funny how she's always telling her kids how much she hates ever having them but will not let anybody treat them bad. They got to the school before Mrs. Vinegar left for the day. Barb didn't know where the class was because she never went to the meetings to meet the teachers. She sent the children to school to get them away from her. She marched straight into the office and demanded to speak to Mr. Bailey right now. The secretary picked up the phone and nervously told Mr. Bailey Mrs. Kingsley wanted to see him right away. He paused a moment hoping it wasn't about Shannon and Miss Belinda again then told her to send her in. As she walked into his office with Sasha in tow the look on her face told him this was not good news. She sat down and immediately began to chew him out about his teacher's behavior with her children. She made Sasha tell him what had been going on in her class. He couldn't believe what he was hearing so he stood up with an angry look on his face and headed to the door. He turned and told Barb he was going to take care of it immediately. He stormed out of the office Barb got up to follow him with Joyce besides her saying, "Now Barb let the principle handle it first calm down." Once she saw the class, he went into she calmly told Joyce, "I'm not going to do anything I'm just going to use the restroom." Joyce stopped walking surprised by Barb's calm demeanor watched her go to the restroom. Joyce looked at Sasha and Val and said, "That went smoother than I expected." But Sasha knew it wasn't over her mom was up to something. Barb came out the restroom and headed towards Joyce and the children she was holding what looked like a clump of paper in her hand from a distance. As she got close Mr. Bailey and Mrs. Vinegar came out and stood in front of the class. Mr. Bailey saw Barb coming towards them holding something in her hand with a paper towel over it but thought nothing of it. Mrs. Vinegar had her back to Barb and was unaware that anybody was behind her she was apologizing to Mr. Bailey for her actions and swearing it would not happen again. Just as Barb got close to them, she pulled the paper towel off a cup in her hand. She proceeded to throw the liquid in the cup on the back of Mrs. Vinegar's dress soaking it. Mrs. Vinegar jumped to the side a little and let out a soft scream and turned to see who wet her dress. Barb stepped up to her and said, "Now you know what it's like to piss on yourself. Mess with my child again and I will hurt you," she turned and headed to the car. Mr. Bailey was shocked and too scared to say anything it happened too fast for him to react. Joyce knew something bad was about to happen once the paper towel came off the cup. She ran towards Barb to try and stop her but was too late the deed had been done. Barb was walking towards the car with a smile on her face. Joyce didn't know if she should stay and apologize or go; she was speechless; she wanted to say something, but nothing would come out. Mrs. Vinegar was in tears not believing what just happened to her again. Joyce turned and ran to the car thinking to herself why I thought I could trust this woman would act normal; now I know she's just crazy. As she got in the car and headed home, she looked over at Barbara who seemed to be perfectly happy with what she did. The children were laughing hysterically.

Joyce smiled and said, "Well I guess she won't be doing that anymore." They both started laughing with the kids as the car pulled out of the parking lot. After having a good laugh Joyce says to Barb, "Could you please give me a warning sign or something the next time you do something like that. You left me standing there looking just as stupid as they were. At least let a sister know something." Barb replied, "If I did that you would've stopped me; besides I don't plan things I just do whatever comes to mind." They all laughed it out as they headed home. Sasha felt proud that her mom came to her rescue just as she did for Shannon it's the first time, she felt she had a normal mom.

CHAPTER THREE

Things weren't so peaceful in the Kingsley house since Barb had to stop working. She started having problems with her pregnancy since the incident at the school. Her doctor told her to stay in bed if she wanted to carry the baby full term. Since then her and James would argue every Friday because she didn't want him taking money from his paycheck for himself. Sometimes Barb would get violent with James hitting him and throwing whatever she could get in her hand at him. Most of the time James would storm out the house to keep from hurting Barb and making her loose the baby. She's not concerned about the baby; there are only two things she cares about money and men in that order. As the arguing increased James was wishing he'd never married her. He left her before when Shannon was small and little James was a baby. He came back because he didn't trust any other woman with his money, and they didn't give him their undivided attention like Barb. He left back then because he claimed Shannon wasn't his child, she came out looking as he put it "high yellow" and he is black. He swore Barb had Shannon from another man; never mind the fact she looked exactly like his niece from his baby sister color and all. Once again here he is married to a woman he doesn't want to be with but need to survive. Shannon always caught the brunt of his frustrations when things were not going good between him and Barb. He would punish her every time Sasha got into something she wasn't supposed to; and Sasha was always getting into something. She is his precious little "stanka" as he called her; he knew she was bad about breaking things she was too small to handle. She looks like his baby sister who is staying with Robert; she is the only child he knows is his as far as he is concerned. Shannon knows her dad doesn't like her much and she can't understand why she is getting punished for Sasha's mess ups. She is beginning to feel like she doesn't belong with her family. Lately she's imagining herself with a good family that loves her;

she starts acting very defiant with James when he would fuss at her over nothing she felt.

It was a Saturday afternoon the first weekend of November and the beginning of Shannon's world being torn apart. She was spending more and more time away from home she either was with Aunt Priscilla or Wanda all day. But this day they were playing in the yard at her house. Gwen was asking why she was always the one getting fussed at all the time. Shannon said to her, "I wish I could run away and never come back. Every time I attempt to, I think who's going to take care of Sasha? Who's going to take care of her when I'm gone? Tears began whelping in her eyes as the desire to not want to live with her family gets stronger. Gwen asked, "Where would go if you do run away?" Shannon looked at her as a tear glides down her face and says, "Far away from here just far away from them." As they are talking Sasha runs in the house to get some water. She didn't let anyone know she wanted it because she wanted to get it herself. She pulled a chair over to the counter, but she was still too short to climb on the countertop. She ran to get her stool out of the bathroom to put in the chair; yep it gave her the extra boost she needed. She stood on top of the counter to open the cabinet door and got a glass out then carefully put it down to close the door. She then put the glass in the sink and turned on the water to fill it. The glass was partially under the water because she didn't want it filling up to the top, but the outside of the glass was wet. It was half full and too heavy for her to hold but she was determined to get her own water. She kneeled down to slowly lift the glass out of the sink to take a drink the glass was shaking as it made its way to her mouth. It was a tall glass and too wide for her hands to hold but she got a drink. Lowering the glass to her chest hugging it with both arms like it was a baby doll; she turned to face the chair to take another drink when it all went wrong. The water came rushing to her face splashing over her eyes then her hands let go of the glass. The sound of glass shattering when it hit the floor was so loud Shannon heard it outside. James came running out the room just as Shannon came through the front door to find out what was going on. They see Sasha on the countertop soak and wet coughing and gasping for air. She looked at them looking at her starts crying and said, "I was getting water and it slipped out of my hand." James was furious and yelled out, "Shannon" not realizing that Shannon was already in the house standing behind him. Shannon surprising herself blurted out, "This is not my fault." James turned to see her behind him yelled back at her, "You're supposed to be watching her little girl and you keep talking back to me I'm gonna whoop your cotton pickin ass right where you stand." At this point Shannon didn't care about the whooping she was going to speak her mind, "She is not my child I didn't have her ya'll did." She quickly ran out the door before James could say or do anything to her. By the time he got to the door to say something she was gone. Shannon was a fast runner he had no idea which direction she had gone. He was furious about the fact that Shannon talked back to him. Barbara came out of the bedroom as James was coming back in the house and slammed the front door. He looked at Barb and said, "I'm tired of that girl you better do something with her, or I will." Barb shook her head and said, "She's just a child James; and why all of a sudden she's being a problem to you?" James angrily yelled, "She ain't none of my child, I don't know who you had her from. The only child I know is mine is Sasha." Barbara looked at him with just as much anger and said, "Well what about the one I'm carrying? Your dumb ass was the one who wanted children I didn't; now you're gonna stand here and own the one you like best. All of them are yours you dumb ass fool! Sasha stood there looking at them both not believing what she was hearing. She began crying as they began yelling at each other louder and louder. They both looked at Sasha crying; they forgot she was in the house. James walked over to her and picked her up. "Don't cry my little stanka daddy's right here for ya hush up now." He called Jr. to come out of the room to clean up the broken glass and water. He walked outside holding Sasha in his arms gently patting her on the back as he walked down the street looking for Shannon. There was no telling who house Shannon went to he turned around and went back home. Sasha was sleep as her head was resting on his shoulder; he walked in the house put her down on the sofa grabbed a few things then walked back out. He had no plans of coming back anytime soon. Shannon ran down to the canal on the back path; she got there and saw Claire sitting at Tate's grave. She went over to sit with her seeing how she hadn't been to Tate's grave since the funeral. Claire saw that she had been crying and asked, "What's wrong Shannon? Someone hurt your feelings? Shannon told Claire everything even the fact that her dad doesn't think she's his child and she's beginning to hate him. Claire looked at her not sure what to say to Shannon; after all she was a bad parent to Tate that's why he's dead now. She took Shannon by the hand and said, "Come with me." They went to Claire's house where she gave her something to eat as they talked getting to know each other better. After eating Shannon sat on the sofa looked around and admired how nice the place looked. She began fantasying how nice life would be for her if she lived here and fell asleep. Claire sat in the chair across from Shannon watching her sleep and praying to the lord. "God please give me a second chance to be a better mother. Kate's children fill her heart with so much love and joy she hates to be away from them. She doesn't know what she's going to do when Kate and Romeo come home; or if they come home. They've been gone for quite some time now since school started. Claire plans to be a permanent figure in the children's life. Shannon woke up from her nap feeling rested; Claire smiled and asked if she was ready to go home. Shannon quickly replied, "No". Claire just said, "Your parents are going to be looking for you, they may be worried." Shannon looked at Claire with a look of assurance and said, "No they're not they don't care about us. I don't know why they even bothered to have children." Claire didn't have the answer or comment for Shannon, but she knew she was right about her parents not caring; she was like that once but not anymore. She wasn't going to make Shannon go home nor was she going out of her way to let Barb know the child was with her. Claire was finding out most of the ladies around her are acting like they are so much better than her when in fact they're lives are just as messed up as hers was. Shannon stayed with Claire Saturday and all-day Sunday; she reluctantly went home Sunday night. She walked in as James and Barbara were sitting at the table eating dinner. Neither of them looked at her; they kept eating acting like they normally do, don't care. Shannon went straight to her room where Sasha was so glad to see her; she started crying and hugged her tight and said, "I missed you so much I thought you were gone for good." Shannon sat on the bed and said, "Sometimes I wish I was gone for good Sasha. They were not worried about me being gone huh?" Sasha shook her head no as a reply. Shannon said, "It figures; did they feed you?" Sasha answered, "No I ate at Mrs. Joyce house before I came home, and Jr. ate at Uncle Roberts. It's no fun here when you are gone next time take me with you; I don't like living with them anymore." Shannon looked at Sasha smiled and kissed her on the forehead. They put on their pajamas and got in bed to go to sleep. Nobody said a word to Shannon about being gone the weekend. James was not too happy about it and was planning on making her pay for it when Barbara isn't around. The week went by smoothly for Shannon. By Wednesday of the following week all hell broke loose on her. Barbara had a late afternoon Dr. appointment something wasn't right with the baby. James knew this was his only chance to get home early and make that girl pay for what she did. Shannon hadn't been home for too long and was already busy helping Sasha with homework. James stepped in the door looking like a crazy man; he rushed up to the table grabbed Shannon by the arm with a tight grip and snatched her out of the chair. Shannon yelled out, "OUCH! You're hurting me; let me go!" He slapped her in the mouth and yelled back, "Shut up don't get sassy with me girl." Sasha started screaming as he dragged Shannon towards the bedroom with her screaming, "Help me Sasha, please help me!" He slammed the door then locked it behind him and threw Shannon on the bed. Just as he leaned over her she kicked him in the face as hard as she could and rolled off the bed before he could grab her again. He yelled out, "Shit, Damn it to hell!" Swirling blood in his mouth from biting his tongue he lunged at Shannon desperate to get a hold of her; but she moved too fast out the way of his grasp. He spit the blood on the floor and mumbled, "You're gonna pay for that little girl," She dodged his grasp and tried to make a run for the door, but he blocked her path. She quickly slides between his legs under the bed using the throw rug to propel her to the other side. She is terrified with fear when she realizes he is not trying to give her a beating but attack her. Sasha is beating on the door screaming and crying thinking it's her fault Shannon is going to get another beating. Shannon is trembling with fear and panic as she tries to stay away from her dad's grip. She runs around the room as fast as she can staying away from corners; he keeps blocking the door and the headboard is blocking the window. She knows sooner or later he's going to catch her, so she screams for Sasha. There's no way out she thinks then out of desperation she yells, "I'm telling mama on you! Just as she tries to dart past him his fingers catch her by the hair. He snatches her back to him and rips off her clothes and pins her down on the bed and angrily says, "Tell her; she ain't gonna believe a word you say." He pulls his pants down and presses his heavy body between her legs then force himself into her small opening. She lets out a scream of terror as the pain makes her small body tremble and her mind goes numb with disbelief that her father is doing this to her. Outside Sasha is frantically trying to find something to save Shannon. She is literally running in circles not knowing what to do until she sees a metal bat leaning on the side of the sofa. She runs over to get it and drags it to the door; it's kind of heavy but she manages to lift it to her shoulder. Just as she does she hear Shannon scream like never before; an urgency of fear took over as she swings the bat to hit the door. The noise of the bat hitting the door was so loud it made James jump up off Shannon before he could do anymore damage to her; he goes to the door prepared to face Barbara. Sasha raises the bat a second time determined she is going to save her sister from the monster. With all her might she swings, and the door opens and the bat hits James in the shin making a clink sound as it makes contact. James falls to the floor screaming grabbing his leg rolling in pain. Shannon sees the door is open muster up the strength to run for it and makes it out; she makes it to her room with Sasha running behind her dragging the bat. Shannon lies on the floor as Sasha stands at the door ready to make another swing at the monster if he comes anywhere near them. Her heart is beating fast from the adrenalin rush going through her body she feels like she can conquer anything. Five minutes has past, and he hasn't come to the door; so, Sasha slowly steps forward to see why. She peeps out first then cautiously steps out in the hallway nothing there. She goes further and sees the door still open; she peeps in to see that he's not there. The room is in shambles she sees blood on the floor and the bed then run back to see what has happened to Shannon; what did he do to make her scream like that? Shannon was in a fetus position on the floor naked crying and shivering uncontrollably saying over and over, "I want to die, I want to die." Sasha ran over to her crying as well; she kneeled down to her sister and held her shivering body and said, "I'm sorry I got you in trouble Shan, I'm sorry I promise I'll be good the next time." Sasha puts a pillow under her head and grabs a blanket to cover her sister. She got little James to fill a small tub with warm water to bring in the room. Sasha goes over and hug's Shannon and say, "Don't leave me Shan please don't leave me." Shannon raise her arm to hug Sasha close to her as the two of them lay there crying. Barbara comes home in time to see little James carrying the tub of water to the bedroom, "Boy where are you going with that water?" Little James was startled by his mom being home so soon he kept walking and said, "Oh mom dad hurt Shannon really bad she need help." Barb dropped her purse on the sofa and went towards the room but was distracted by the mess of her own bedroom as she slowed down to look in. Her heart sank to her feet as she saw the blood on the bed and floor. She wanted to cry then but rushed to the kids' room to see how bad it was with Shannon. She came in as Sasha was starting to bathe Shannon, she almost did not recognize Shannon. Her face was swollen and bruised as was her body bruised and she noticed the blood between her legs. Barb backed out of the room as her mind went in chaos at the sight of her child; the voices started taking over her mind telling her how this is going to ruin her marriage. She went back to the door as Shannon called out to her, "Mommy daddy hurt my inside really bad." Barbara backs out of the room again covering her mouth with her hands as tears rolls down her face. She runs to the bathroom to throw up sickened by the sight of a broken innocent child. Her mind is spinning stuck on one thought, "This is not happening to me" it repeats over and over again. She sits on the bathroom floor and began to wail loud out of control. Sasha don't know what to do, Shannon usually calms their mom down when she gets like that. Sasha managed to get Shannon off the floor onto the bed. Little James put the tub of water on the floor by the bed; Sasha took a sponge and soap and began bathing her sister ever so gentle being careful not to cause her any more pain. Crying Sasha says to Shannon, "It's okay Shan I'll take care of you." Sasha wipes over the bruised areas then pats them dry with a towel apologizing to Shannon again thinking she caused this to happen to her sister. Shannon manage to shake her head and whispers, "It's not your fault Sasha; you did not do this to me." Sasha was doing good bathing her sister until it came to cleaning between her legs where the blood was now dry and sticky. Shannon wouldn't let Sasha touch her down there at first, she thought it was going to be too painful. Sasha didn't understand why the blood was down there, but she was brave enough to clean it off when Shannon allowed her to. She made her brother empty the tub as she dressed Shannon and helped her lay back in the bed. The house was quiet; little James came to the door and said, "Mom is gone." Sasha went to see if she was in her room, but no one was there. Once again, they were home alone to tend to themselves. Sasha went back in the room to tell Shannon they were alone, "No one is here with us again so I'm going to see if I can get us something to eat, I'll be back." Before she could step away from the bed Shannon grabbed her by the arm and sat up looking scared and shaking with fear; "No please don't leave me he might come back." Sasha never saw her sister act like this before she was starting to get scared too but answered calmly, "Okay I'll stay with you." Shannon calmed down then lay back on the bed. Sasha went in the bathroom and saw a bottle of children's aspirin and a cup of water on the countertop; she figured her mom got it down to give to Shannon but never came back to the room. Sasha took two of the little orange pills and water to Shannon to take. Shannon chewed the sweet orange pills then drank the water then lay down to go to sleep hoping when she wakes up this was just a terrible dream. Sasha got a book and began reading to Shannon as she lay in the bed; listening to Sasha read made Shannon feel proud. She began imagining herself in the story to escape the pain of what just happened. Sasha was halfway through the story when she heard the front door open and close; she put the book down then ran to see who it was. Barbara was back with some food; Sasha ran up to her and asked, "Is that for us? I am really hungry." Barbara looked down at her and said, "Yes, it is have a seat while I fix you and little James a plate." Sasha ran to the table then turned and asked, "What about Shannon? You have something for her too?" Barb replied, "Don't worry baby I have some soup I'm going to feed her, eat up now." She took a cup of soup to the room not sure if Shannon will eat any of it after what she been through. A sick feeling came over her as sees Shannon swollen bruised face; she was afraid to touch her at first, her mind didn't want to deal with what happened. She forced herself to give Shannon a gentle nudge, "Wake up Shannon try to put something in your stomach," she spoke softly. Shannon opened her eyes surprised to see her mom standing by the bed with food for her. She slowly sat up as her mom sat on the edge of the bed and slowly began feeding her the soup. Barb didn't know what to say to her daughter she just silently fed her the soup one spoon full at a time until it was gone. She couldn't bring herself to ask what happened she could see most of it. She was fearful of what she didn't see; her mind couldn't absorb the reality of the fact that she married a horrible man. Her hands started trembling at the thought of that and the voices in her head started talking. "She did it, she did it to herself you know; she just wants to break up my marriage." The voices repeated over and over louder and louder. Shannon took the cup and spoon out of her mom's hands as she noticed the crazy look appearing on her face. She's seen that look too many times to know that something evil is brewing in her mom's head. Shannon spoke softly her mom, "It's okay now I've had enough to eat." Barb quickly got up and ran out of the room as fast as she could. She ran into her bedroom and slammed the door and began screaming and yelling to herself. Objects were being tossed around as she yelled, "Shut-up, just shut-up." The children were used to this behavior from their mom they knew to stay out of her way. Sasha finished eating and went in the bathroom to run some water to take a bath she was feeling tired emotionally than physical. It was too much for a six-year-old to take in one day; all she wants to do now is go to bed and tomorrow will be better. Just as she started the water running Shannon came in the bathroom to help; but Sasha wanted to prove that she was big enough to do it herself. "Oh no Shannon I can bathe myself go back to bed." Shannon tried to make her swollen lips smile but it was too painful she answered, "You can't get out of the tub wet by yourself Sasha you'll slip and fall. I can't let you get hurt so I'm going to help you; besides you helped me more than you know." Sasha agreed and said, "Okay I really didn't want to be in here alone anyway." Little James came in the back door he had left after bringing Sasha the tub of water. He heard his mom screaming and yelling in her room he went to the bathroom door; he was surprised to see Shannon up, "Let me guess, she saw what he did to you and can't deal with it." Sasha angrily said, "That was not nice Junior you take it back right now." He looked at Shannon and said, "I'm sorry Shan I didn't mean to make fun of it all." Shannon held back the tears then asked him, "Where were you all this time? He answered, "I went to play with Red man then went to Uncle Robert to eat dinner; Auntie asked about ya'll I told her ya'll were busy cleaning up. I'm full auntie cooked a good meal. Sasha told him, "Mom fixed you a plate it's on the table I guess she'll eat it herself." James ran to the table; the girls came out of the bathroom and saw him sitting at the table eating again. Shannon laughed and said, "I thought you were full, boy you're just greedy." They went in the room and climbed into bed they were not concerned about their mom having crazy fits as they called them.

It was getting late and Barbara was still up waiting for James to come home. Questions kept flowing through her mind; what will I say to him? What can I do to him? Is my marriage over? Why did he do that to her? She got up and went into the living room and sat in the darkness. "I don't want to be by myself," she mumbled. The baby moved slightly giving a weak kick then nothing there was a little pain but not much. She looks down at her stomach and says, "I never wanted children my mom and dad made me get married. I wouldn't be in this mess if it wasn't for them." She sat in the darkness weighing her options. She always chooses the man over the child; money and men are all that matters to her in that order. James didn't come home that night he went to his brother and slept on the sofa. He knew there would be hell to pay from his wife for what he did; but he didn't feel bad about it he felt he had every right to do it. His wife didn't care for her why should he. He was drunk and fell fast asleep as the thoughts quickly vanished away. As morning came Shannon was up early getting Sasha dressed for school she cooked her some breakfast and sent her out to catch the bus; she was in a lot of pain but owed her little sister her best for getting her away from that monster. Junior got dressed shoveled down the breakfast and ran to Eddy's house to meet Red man. Shannon wasn't going to school until her face healed, she wasn't the same little girl after what happened yesterday. She still felt dirty and broken every time the images popped in her mind and would run to the bathroom to wash her hands. She stayed in her room with a chair propped against the door in case her dad tried to come in while she was sleep; the chair would give her a chance to run away. She got dressed then got back in bed and was sleep for twenty minutes and was awakened by loud voices. She sat up in the bed to listen making sure she wasn't having a bad dream. She knew it wasn't a dream when they came in the kitchen and the yelling got louder. Barbara was so upset and crying again. Shannon knew by the sound of her mom's voice she was not in her right mind; when she's that person she is very violent not even James can control her. Shannon quietly slides the chair away from the door to peep out to see what is happening. Barbara has a knife her hand pointing it at James threatening to kill him. He keeps his distance from her not wanting her to get more enraged than what she already is. Barb is also bent over holding her stomach as if she is in pain. She stands up straight then lunges at James with the knife then starts having epileptic convulsions; James grabs the knife from her as he tries to hold her still. Her body is shaking so violently James loses his grip and she falls into the wall creating a big hole, but it helps to control her. James gets a spoon in her mouth to keep her from swallowing her tongue. As she lay there her eyes began to roll back in her head to where you could only see the white. James panics and yells out to Shannon, "Go get Joyce we need to get your mom to the hospital." He didn't know Shannon had already darted out the back door going to get Joyce when she saw her mom bending over in pain. Halfway to Joyce house she stopped and thought about how bruised up her face looked but the thought her mom could die made her start back running. Joyce was standing out in the driveway as Shannon rushed up to her and said, "Mom needs to go to the hospital quick she's going to die!" Joyce looked at Shannon's face horrified by what she saw she screams, "Oh my God! What happened to you? Shannon looked at Joyce wanting to tell everything but there was no time for that now she just said, "I'll tell you later I promise mom needs help right now!" Joyce ran and got purse and keys then they both jumped in the car. They come in the front door as James calls out Shannon's name for the second time as Barbara lay in his arms limp not responding to his calls. He picks her up and rushes her to Joyce car they speed away to the hospital. She waited in the lobby with Shannon as James walked alongside the bed as they wheel Barb back to perform emergency surgery as she started hemorrhaging as he brought her in. An hour later the Dr. comes to talk to James about Barb; "she is stable but we have to transfer her to Miami to have a more serious surgery there; the baby is dead inside and there is damage to the womb she may die but she cannot have any more children. James was happy to hear she couldn't have any more kids; he rode in the ambulance with her to Miami. Joyce took Shannon home to her house her husband Greg was there unpacking and glad to be home. He has a few weeks to spend with the family before he is off to travel again. Of course, for Joyce that means no sneaking out to meet Romeo who's been gone longer than usual. Greg took one look at Shannon and yelled out, "What the hell happened to you?" Shannon was scared to say anything at first then she thought; I hate him anyway I don't care about what happens to him. She blurted out the whole story like she had diarrhea at the mouth, once she started talking, she couldn't stop the words from coming out. By the time she finished Greg wished he'd never asked but was glad he did. He left the room madder than a grizzly; made a few phone calls then left the house. Joyce was in tears holding one hand over her mouth to keep from screaming. She walked over to Shannon and gently held her in her arms softly saying, "You poor baby, you poor baby. This shouldn't have happened to someone as sweet as you. You don't deserve this; you don't deserve this." Shannon was relieved to finally get that out in the open but the feeling of being dirty overcame her and she needed to wash her hands. As Shannon went to the bathroom to wash her hands Joyce went to look for Greg. When he wasn't in his office she checked outside, and his car was gone. She was trying to remember if he was in shock or angry when he left. She couldn't recall or concentrate on anything she was feeling so much pain and anger. She didn't know what else to say to Shannon to make things better for her. When Shannon came from the bathroom Joyce walked over to her to hug her again this time Shannon cries with her.

Greg went to the bar not far from the neighborhood meeting all the men on the street. He told them everything Shannon told him. They were not planning on calling the police, oh no; but they were going to make James wish they had called the police when they get through with him. Most of the men wanted to kill him but Greg said, "Nah man, I don't want any of us spending life in prison for a piece of shit like him. Let's just make sure he wears a good ass kicking he won't forget; and make sure every household with a child knows what he is except his brother that bastard might be just like him we'll keep an eye on him too. They calmed down and agreed to do what Greg suggested then had a few drinks and went home. Shannon, Sasha and little James stayed over to Joyce until their dad came home from Miami. Greg had Shannon leave a note telling her dad to come pick them up from Joyce house when he gets home. James stayed at the hospital a few days with Barbara not out of love; he knew by now questions are being asked what happened to Shannon. He needed time to come up with a good lie to discredit whatever Shannon had said. He was being very helpful with the hospital staff taking care of Barbara's every need. The nurses thought he was the most loving husband a woman could ever have. Barbara would be in the hospital a few more weeks to recover fully from her ordeal; she was still having small seizures and had to stay sedated to keep from hurting herself. James stayed with her for four days he needed to get home and get back to work. Robert picked up his brother from the hospital because he wanted to see how Barbara was doing. The ride back to Boynton was intense, they argued all the way back; Robert knew James did something to put Barb in the hospital he just didn't know what it was. He knows his brother and was trying to get it out of him to no avail; James wasn't telling him anything he figured he was safe since Robert didn't know which means Shannon kept her mouth shut. Robert took James home and didn't say another word to him as he got out of the car and pulled away mad as a hornets' nest. The house was dark as he steps in no sign of the children anywhere. He goes in the room to find a note on the bed. He tries to read it and gets mad at himself for not staying in school. He crumbles the letter in his hand and throws it in the trash can. He figures there's one other place the children will be besides Robert's. His heart starts beating fast from fear as he realizes he has to go to Greg's house to get them. He attempts to calm his nerves and get his story together as he gets close to Greg's house. He's not sorry for what he did to Shannon; he's afraid someone will find out and try to stop him from doing it again. As he thinks about it, he intends to finish what he started with Shannon. He knocks on the door with his big heavy fist. Greg peeps out to see its James and the anger began to swell inside him. He calms himself down before he opens the door; a fake smile appears on his face as the door swings open. "Hey James, man what's up? How's your wife doing; heard she's in the hospital?" James was surprised Greg was home he was expecting Joyce to come to the door. His heart started beating so fast and hard it felt like it was about to come out of his chest. Nervously he said, "I ugh came to take the kids home, how ya doin man? It's ugh been a while since I last saw ya." Greg kept smiling and said, "Yeah it has, you know me always out making money to take care of the family. Come on in and have a seat tell me about your wife; is she okay?" James really didn't want to sit around and answer questions he just wanted to get out of there. Being polite he sat down and told how Barb was going to be in the hospital for a few more weeks, she lost the baby. Greg decided now was the time to put his plan in motion. "I'm sorry to hear that man I just got back home; I was getting the fellows together to meet up at the bar for some drinks. Just want to catch up on what I missed while I was gone, come and join us drinks on me. Before you say it, Joyce don't mind the kids staying another night, she loves having them over." James accepted the invitation with a smile on his face thinking all was clear and there was nothing to worry about. "Yeah man, I'll go with you guys I could use a few drinks right about now it's been a rough week for me." In his mind Greg yelled gottcha! He said to James, "Great! I'll let my wife know we're leaving." He told Joyce the plan was in motion and kissed her. All the men came out of their houses at the same time to meet in the middle of the street to discuss where they were going for drinks. After fifteen minutes of talking they decided to walk down to the canal and sit in the park the children built. They had coolers filled with beer and liquor with large plastic cups. They all were thinking the same thing except James. It's a perfect place for a good ass kicking and no one would hear you screaming; there were lots of talking and laughing until they reached the spot. All of a sudden it was so quiet the only noise you heard was the crickets. James looked around to see what was going on that would cause the guys to get so quiet; but before he could figure it out, he was hit in the jaw. The licks started coming from all directions before he could react to one. While he was falling to the ground, he heard someone say, "This is for the pain your daughter felt from you bitch ass punk. You ain't man enough to handle a woman huh." He hit the ground hard as fists were pounding him from every direction then the kicking and stomping started. They were careful not to break any bones, they just wanted to have the pleasure of making him feel as much pain and agony as he gave to Shannon. Greg wanted to kill him, but Daniel pulled him away to calm him down. They all stopped walked over to the coolers and poured themselves a drink. Daniel saluted a toast, "To Family!" They all replied, "Here, here!" James lay there moaning in pain as Greg walked over to him and said, "Yo man this is your only warning, touch any child again you're a dead man." They sat around drinking and talking a little longer, every time James would try to get up somebody would go and knock him back down. They started talking about Romeo and his wife leaving their kids home alone now for months. Daniel didn't say a word about the situation because he was taking care of the kids, he didn't want anyone to know that yet. Stanley was the mysterious rich man who lived in the mansion across from the graveyard. No one knew how he became so rich; they never bothered to ask because he so active in the community, he made things happen. Stan said he would hire an investigator to find out where Romeo and his wife be going for so long that they can't take their kids with them. "They have no sense of love for those children to be parents, they don't need them." Bryon quickly asked, "Man what we gone do? Ya'll know how Romeo is, that dude crazy as fuck man. The way he treat women is something crucial. He's gonna kill somebody one of these days; the only reason he ain't done his wife is because she got all that money her parents left her." Skip joined in by saying, "He touch one of ours he's a dead man, there's no beat down for him he's gone be dead." Skip knew Romeo and Joyce has a thang going on, but he was not about to tell Greg or anyone else for that matter. He had been following Joyce to make sure she makes it back home safe; he didn't trust Romeo with her. Greg is like a brother to him and Joyce is like a sister. They were silent for a moment contemplating on what other option they had besides killing him. No one wanted to kill him, but Romeo was the type that when confronted with any issue, you either had to kill him or he was going to kill you. Daniel interrupted the silence by saying, "Hey ya'll, let's wait until after the holidays to deal with Romeo, none of us is ready to have blood on our hands right now." They all agreed to wait until after the holidays to do Romeo. They let James get up after he promised not to tell a sole about what he heard; he didn't like Romeo either. They left the graveyard with a new mission in mind, Romeo. Daniel went home and told Claire about the guys looking to find out where Romeo and Kate be going, that was all he was telling her. Their plan is to get the children, which is why they got the empty lot across the street and building a big house on it. The plan is in motion for them to start over with being better parents.

James slowly made his way home every step was painful. He couldn't believe it; how could he have been such a fool into thinking no one would notice what had been done to Shannon? One thing was clear to him; he couldn't put one finger on Shannon while they live here. He mumbles out loud, "I'll just move to another city; who she gone tell then?"

Shannon was glad to be spending another night with Joyce she got to spend more time with her friend. Wanda cried when she saw the bruises on Shannon's body; she made Shannon talk about how she feels inside. Shannon told her she always feels dirty and broken where nobody can fix her. She ran and washed her hands three times and started sucking food residue off her teeth making sure they felt smooth and clean. She didn't know she had developed compulsive behaviors to deal with her pain inside; she just called it "Broken". At home James was feeling like he was broken, every inch of his body was in pain. He believed Greg when he said he would kill him if he touched a child again. But a pervert is going to be a pervert unless you lock them up or kill them. He has to behave while living here so he decided to start looking for jobs in other cities far away from here. Yes, he still plans to make Shannon pay for telling on him; what a sick pervert indeed.

Skip wasn't the only one who knew Romeo and Joyce; Claire told Daniel about the secret meetings. They really have to be careful now with the kids she doesn't want Joyce to get caught in the crossfire of Romeo's wrath. "That man is a dangerous natural born killer," she warns Daniel. That was of no concern to Daniel, "I know he is babe, but Joyce put herself in harm's way the moment she started the affair. If she continues the affair, she stands a chance of being killed by him; she's a grown woman, she knows what she's doing." Daniel can't believe he's plotting with his wife to take somebody's children from them. He didn't want Claire to get involved with the children until he found out they were Romeo's; now he knows Joyce is a piece in the puzzle. Daniel has hated Romeo from way back, they vowed the next time they meet one of them will die. He can't tell Greg about Joyce affair; it would blow their chance at getting the children and that would break Claire's heart. Her happiness means everything to him; he no longer feels guilty about having the kids with them. If it wasn't for him and Claire those children will be starving. The children are in love with Daniel and Claire so much they are calling them mom and papa. Daniel and Kenny have developed a father son bond, the one thing he didn't have with Tate. He didn't think Kenny would accept him as a father in their lives; but Kenny desperately needed a man to talk to. He was afraid he would grow up not knowing how to be a man or a father. Kenny and Stacy really appreciated Claire giving them the opportunity to go to school. They made the best of it by becoming straight 'A' students fearing they mom may come back at any time and take them out again. Claire encouraged them and helps them set goals and not give up on them. They felt more at home with Claire than with their own parents. When their parents did come home it seemed like they were spending time with distant relatives. It was getting to the point where they couldn't wait for them to leave so they could go back to Claire. Kenny and Stacey decided it was time to take matters in their own hands in determining what was best for the family. Three weeks ago, he obtained a legal guardian form and put a fake field trip permission form on top with a slip of carbon paper under the signature line. He carefully lined it up with the signature line on the legal guardianship form. Kate signed it without reading it she didn't care what was going on in school she just wanted him out of her face. Now Kenny just has to get Daniel and Claire to sign it and get it notarized. Kenny is making sure they won't be going to a foster home with strangers when Stacey tells D.C.F their parents have abandoned them. Kenny's been researching their situation and wants to be a lawyer to help children like them. He decided this was the time to talk to Daniel and Claire about what is to be done with them. Daniel and Claire were sitting at the table trying to come up with a better plan to get family services involved without anyone knowing they are taking care of the children. Kenny came in and asked, "Pops, can I talk to ya'll for a minute?" Daniel replied, "Sure son have a seat." Kenny presented the form to them and said, "I had my mom to sign this because I don't want us taken away from you. Reading the heading at the top of the form has Claire heart beating fast from fear and excitement; she couldn't believe what she was seeing, it made her speechless at first. All Daniel could say was, "Wow, honey…. what the…. why we didn't think of this?" Claire finally asked,

"Kenny how did you get this?" With a smile on his face Kenny answered, "Oh getting the form was easy; and getting mom to sign it was even easier." He said with a bigger smile on his face, he was proud of what he'd accomplished. "All you guys need to do is get it notarized and we'll be able to be a real family without hiding." They looked at each other as Daniel said, "This might work." Before Claire could say anything Kenny excitedly declared, "Of course it will work dad! As soon as Stacey informs D.C.F that we have been abandoned it's going to work out just fine!" Claire panicked and said, "Isn't it too soon? I mean, we have other things to consider; what about waiting until after the holidays, (Hinting at Daniel about the plan to take care of Romeo). Daniel smiling with excitement said, "Calm down babe, this is going to help things fall in our favor we have nothing to worry about. I know someone who can notarize these papers for us." He hugged Kenny tight and said, "Thank you Jesus! Claire said with hands raised high and tears flowing down her face, "Thank you lord for allowing this to work in our favor, I give you the glory." Kenny was just as happy as they were; he thought it was going to take some convincing to get them to take the form. Little did he know he just made a hard situation get that much easy. They told Kenny not to let the others know until after everything is done. He easily agreed considering he didn't tell them about his plans. After Kenny left, they picked up the conversation about the new house being built which should be ready to move into by December, which are only a few weeks away. How Thanksgiving goes depends on whether or not if Kate's going to be home with the kids. Everything must seem the same or the chances of them becoming a family will be lost forever. Kate came home for two days then left. The children were sad whenever their parents were home with them; not because things were bad for them there (which they were) but because they missed being loved by Claire. Claire had baby Queen spoiled so much so that she didn't like being held by her own mom. Kenny and Stacey assured the others that they only have to endure this for a little while longer; everyone must play they're role if they want a permanent life with Daniel and Claire. No one wanted to be without Daniel and Claire they were willing to do whatever it took to be with them, even turn in their own parents for neglecting them. The children had their own plans going in motion; getting school counseling started which is going to alert D.C.F to investigate the family. Little did they know once D.C.F gets involved it's going to open up a whole new can of worms for Romeo and Kate. They don't know their dad is a potential killer, all they know is he's never there for them.

Greg gets home and tells Joyce about the serious ass kicking they put on James. He goes into telling her about their plans to look into Romeo and Kate leaving the kids home alone all the time. Joyce heart skipped a beat and felt like it fell to her feet. She almost chocked on her drink. Greg leaned over and gave her pat on the back, "You okay honey?" All she could do was shake her head yes; a little of the liquid got in her windpipe. As she coughs it out, she panics and says in her mind, "Oh shit, I can't let him find out about us! Damn its Romeo! Why ya'll stupid ass won't stay home with ya'll kids! Calm down Joyce, calm down; you're gonna give yourself away." She quickly gathered her wits together and started asking questions to get the details of the plan. "So, when are you guys gonna start looking into that?" Greg sat back in the chair after seeing she was okay and said, "I don't know; Stan said he's gonna take care of that for us. I think he said something about hiring a P.I." Joyce almost stopped breathing at the sound of that. She knew she would have to stay away from Romeo until this P.I. thing blows over. Sounding serious Greg said, "The moment we find out something we're gonna have to confront him honey." Looking at her face to face he finish by saying, "And when we do; we're gonna have to kill him. I'm just letting you know in case the police come knocking." Joyce nervously warns her husband, "Baby please don't get too involved in this; you're not a killer. Greg puts his drink down and grabs Joyce hand and says, "Every man has the ability to kill, you just got to know what button to push. When it comes to Romeo you either kill him or he'll kill you. I will put his ass down so fast; he won't have time to think about raising a hand to kill me. You better believe that." He got up and left Joyce sitting by herself. Fear overtakes her as she realizes her husband is contemplating on killing her lover and it's not over her. She knows Greg is right about Romeo, and there's no way for her to warn him without getting caught. She went to the room to try and talk Greg out of killing any man. "Greg, please rethink this; back away from this plan please." Greg sat on the bed looking up at his wife as if she lost her mind. Angrily he said, "What you want me to do Joyce? Stand by and watch them starve their children to death? He nearly killed a prostitute the last time he was home. The only reason he hasn't killed Kathryn is because she controls the money. They have millions of dollars and can't... no, won't take care of their children. I have a problem with that Joyce. I'm not going to stand by and watch children die when I know I can do something to stop it. I'm just going to tell him to step up and be a man and take care of his family." She saw that he was very angry at her for asking him to step back she then said, "Look just let the authorities handle it is all I'm asking you to do." Greg angrily pushes himself up off the bed turns to say to Joyce, "Let me help you understand something Joyce; Kate can make those children situation disappear before the authorities can do anything and the abuse will just start all over for them. At least my way they will be in a win, win situation." Greg went to the wet bar to pour himself a strong drink to calm himself down. Joyce knew Greg's mind was made up when it comes to doing the right thing; there was no talking him out of it. She realized seeing Romeo was no longer an option; she'll have to keep her distance until all of this is over.

Thanksgiving was upon everyone before they knew it; the last few months have been an emotional roller coaster for the adults. Barbara came home to a strange acting husband; he took the kids shopping and bought new shoes and clothes for each one. He filled the kitchen pantry with groceries then went out and bought new furniture. Barb had mixed feelings around James, and she could no longer trust him around Shannon. When she left the house, the children were with her at all times. She loved the holidays (the parties mainly) she was a much nicer person during the holiday seasons. Joyce became Barbs best friend since Joyce been staying home on the weekends. She wanted to ask Joyce why she was hanging around the house these past weekends but decided to just enjoy hanging out with her friend. Barb and Joyce decided to have Thanksgiving dinner together at Joyce house. It started out with two families enjoying eating food together; but it grew into a neighborhood holiday party at Joyce house. Every family would bring food to cut down on the time spent in the kitchen for the women. They want to spend time planning black Friday shopping strategies. Even though Stanley has a big mansion with enough space for them, Greg's house has the largest yard for the children to roam and play. They didn't want the children to ruin the beautiful manicured grass at Stan's house. The men plan to watch the games drink their booze and say yes to whatever the women ask them to do for less aggravation. Stanley arranged to have a large pavilion tent be put up beside the house with tables and chairs in case it rains they will be covered, and no mud will be tracked in the house.

The pool was covered to prevent accidental drowning; it was a warm Thanksgiving and no swimming was allowed. The adults were ready to eat, drink and be merry. The children were just happy to be out of school; plus, it was a holiday to show off cousins to friends. The surprise of the season was when Romeo and Kate came and got their kids and took them away with them. Eddy and Red man were scared to go; they thought their parents were coming to take them away for good to be a family. They felt they already had that with Daniel and Claire, giving them up was not an option. Kenny and Stacey calmed them all down and said to them, "It's only for the holidays ya'll, don't show our hand yet. If it's over a week then start worrying." A limo came to pick them up and take them to the airport. Kate bought a house in the Jamaican Islands. She wanted to spend Thanksgiving on the islands with the children for a few days; that's about as long as she can stand to be around them. She never imagined herself growing up to treat her kids the way her parents treated her. She shook the thought of that off and boarded the plane with no intent to change what she was doing to them. She felt that life wasn't good to her why make it good for them. Kathryn wasn't too heartless towards the children; she had her lawyer draw up a will leaving everything she has to them should anything happen to her; the one thing Romeo knows nothing about. He almost killed her twice when she had nothing, and she hasn't trusted him since; the money is the only thing keeping her alive and she knows it. Having a Thanksgiving dinner in a luxurious lifestyle was her idea. She wanted to know how they would handle themselves living like rich people. The children didn't know what to expect from their parents on this trip. They were nervous and afraid thinking they were being taken away from Claire. When they got to the house, they all gathered in one room not saying a word. Kate thought they were afraid of being in a strange place, or maybe they just were not used to being in a nice clean house; she chuckled a little at that thought. Kenny called them together to make sure no one overreacts or panic. "Guys we're going to be fine. I promise they are not going to put up with us more than seven days, so chill. Let's act like we normally would while we're with them; we don't want them to know things have changed for us, Jamar and Red man be ya'll usual bad selves." They all laughed, and group hugged.

Dinner was delicious because she hired a chef to cook it the day before; she wasn't planning on being that good of a mom and cook for them. On the next day the children spent most of their time on the beach they never saw that much water before. It was so blue and clear they could see the bottom; they were even chasing the fish trying to catch them with their hands. Kate called them in to eat dinner; the table was beautifully set with fall decorations and food. They ate so much till they were stuffed like a turkey. Never had they had that much food placed before them and could eat as much as they wanted. They had to admit so far, they were having a blast with mom and dad. No one was thinking about being scared or cautious; Kate took them skating, bike riding, zip line and shopping. She even arranged for them to spend time on her yacht. Jamar and Red man were having fun running from one side of the cabin to the other. Romeo finally yelled at them to stop running; it seemed like his voice roared so loud it shook the rafters. Then reality set in, everyone snapped at attention as the deep voice commanded. The boys stopped running and quickly walked over to Kenny with their eyes stretched as wide as quarters and their hearts beating a hundred miles an hour; at least that's what it felt like to them. They just knew their dad was coming over to slap the stupid out of them, but he didn't even move an inch out of his chair. They gathered in a bunch and quickly went to the upper deck where they stayed enjoying the view of the ocean. Eddy broke the silence when she said, "I miss mama Claire, at this time of the day she's doing my hair and answering all my questions without getting angry at me for asking; I love her for that." Kenny cuts in with, "Pops Daniel is so proud of me for being smart, he doesn't tell me to shut up when I discover something new. I love him for helping me understand how important a man is to his family." One by one they all expressed their love for Daniel and Claire then watched the sun set. The boat finally made its way back to dock; once it was tied off the children quickly exited the boat and noisily ran to shore. Red man and Jamar were as usual two peas in a pod getting in trouble. Kate screamed and yelled out, "That's it I'm taking ya'll bad asses back tomorrow pack ya'll shit when ya get in the house." The boys ran to catch up with others to tell them the good news. "We're leaving tomorrow ya'll, they yelled out as they approached. No one asked why they just took off running towards the house with baby in tow as fast as they could to begin packing; they lasted five days. Stacey looked at Kenny with a smile on her face and said, "You were right." They were so happy to be leaving they turned packing into a game, a very noisy game. They were so loud it made Kate come running up to yell, "Hurry the hell up ya'll getting out of here tonight. The limo is on its way I can't take another hour of this." She walked off waving one hand in the air shaking her head side to side mumbling to herself. They were quiet but giggled softly and finished packing clothes in the new luggage she bought for their new clothes. Within thirty minutes the children and the luggage's were outside waiting for the car. Of course, Kate and Romeo were staying on the island, but she arranged for them to fly home on her private jet with a limo waiting at the airport to take them home. She convinced herself she didn't hate her children; she couldn't stand to be around them. The driver loads the children and the luggage in the car and drives them to the airport. He lets up the window that separates the front from the back and makes a call. "Yeah Stanley, it's me Doug; I got everything you need man. On my way back I'll see you in a few hours. He boarded the plane with the children and went to the cock pit to fly them home. They land at the Miami airport where he loaded them again in the limo there and drove them home. He made sure they were safely in the house then he drove up to talk to Stanley. He showed Stanley pictures of the house, yacht and plane she owned in Jamaica. He handed him records all her purchases along with pictures of their activities. Doug was known to be the best P.I money can buy. He once worked for the F.B.I but quit after giving them twenty years of his life. He decided to become a private investigator it was safer, and he was tired of being alone. He kept in close contact with his friends in case he needed help in high places. He allowed them to use him on occasions for some cases undercover as payment for some hard to get information for some of his clients. Doug handed over phone records, bank statements, and trust fund statements. Lucky for him Kate's lawyer was a friend who owed him a favor. He wasn't surprised about the will, but what made him choke was stumbling on the filing of guardianship papers that Daniel and Claire signed and notarized with Kate's signature while she was in Jamaica. Stanley was shocked at first because Daniel never mentioned to anyone that he was planning on taking the children in any of the meetings. Doug asked Stan if he wanted him to look into it further. Stanley told him, "No it looks like everything's falling into place for them. They'll get what they want; but not the way they want it." He paid Doug a well-deserved lump sum of money and sent him out. He sat there for a little while thinking to himself; it's going to be an interesting new year after all if things don't come to a head before then. He locked the information in his safe and went to bed.

Joyce was sitting outside in the dark when the limo pulled up across the street. Her heart started beating with excitement as she watched the children come out one by one hoping to get a glance at Romeo. She wanted so badly to warn him about what was coming his way, but she would risk losing all that was important to her. She saw no adult get out of the car other than the driver unloading the luggage. When he finished and got back in the car her heart sank down in her stomach from sadness; but almost leaped out of her chest from fear when she saw him go to Stanley's house. She stood up and paced back and forth then stopped and said, "Shit! Quietly, but angry at herself for not paying attention to what the driver looked like. Fear overcame her as her gut feeling was telling her that was the P.I Stan hired. She pressed her stomach in tight, moaned and sat down. She rocked back and forth telling herself to calm down. She didn't know what to think and Greg wasn't telling her what was being said in the meetings anymore. She overstepped her bounds with him trying to protect her lust for another man rather than the lives and wellbeing of children. Not only is he not telling her things, he's beginning to question her mood swing. She misses sneaking out to meet Romeo; mainly the wild sex they have. Romeo acts like a maniac and it seems to draw Joyce into a world of uncontrollable passion that she now longs for. Greg's beginning to notice the difference when they have sex, she's acting like she's not satisfied with him. She even tried some of the moves on him, but he wasn't into rough sex. She was pushy about it at first until he started asking where she was learning the moves from; she lied and said she got them from watching porn movies. Joyce knows When Greg suspects something he's going to hang around until he finds out what it is; another reason why she's been home instead of out in the clubs. The limo passed leaving the neighborhood; she got up and went inside. She decided there was nothing she could do but wait it out; she'll see Romeo when it's safe.

As soon as Doug left the children ran out the back door heading over to see Daniel and Claire. They couldn't wait to tell them how their Thanksgiving went with their parents. They passed by the new house that was being built; it was almost finished. They turned around to go and peep through the windows. It had beautiful dark hardwood flooring though out, the appliances were still in boxes waiting to be installed. Stacey said, "I wonder whose house this is? It sure looks nice inside." Kenny who usually knows everything replied, "I don't know, somebody with good taste in what they want in a house." They all said, "Yeah;" at the same time laughed, walked away to cross the street. It was late at night, but they didn't want to spend another night without Claire. Kenny banged on the door hard to make sure Daniel would wake up. He came to the door angrily yelled out, "Who is it?" Sounding like a group choir they answered, "It's us we're back!" Daniel opened the door and was almost knocked down with hugs. He asked, "When did you guys get back?" Stacey blurted out before anyone could answer, "Just now, where's mom? We miss you guys so much." "Yeah a whole bunch," chimed in the little ones. Daniel smiled and said, "Well considering it's late I'd say she's in bed sleep." Before he could say or do anything else, they all ran in the room jumped in the bed smothering Claire with hugs and kisses. Queen was sleeping through all the commotion as Kenny laid her in the crib. He and Daniel stayed in the living room doing some man bonding. After telling Claire how much they never wanted to leave her again the little ones fell asleep in bed next to her. Daniel and Kenny came in to help Claire and Stacey put them to bed. They stayed up two hours longer talking to Kenny and Stacey who mentioned how beautiful the house across the street looked inside and out. Stacey asked, "Whose is it being built for mom?" Claire just shrugged her shoulders up as if to say she had no clue. They decided not to tell anybody about the house until they knew for sure they could get the children permanently. They plan to get the Department of Children and Family Services involved just before school break for Christmas; that is if Kate and Romeo aren't back by then. They've been staying away from the children longer lately; it's as if they're deliberately making it easy for the kids to be taken from them. How could parents act so cold towards their children, Claire thought to herself. Then she said out loud, "You did it to yours Claire when you were strung out so don't judge." Stacey asked, "Done what mom?" Claire shook it off and said, "It's late let's talk about it when the sun rise."

The smell of coffee brewing woke Daniel up; he rolled over to feel the pillow on the other side of the bed. "Hmm, no wife; it figures she would be the first to get up," he mumbles to himself. He lifts his head to peep over at the clock and sees it is 5a.m. He then pushed himself up to get a closer look and says, "Yep, five; ya gotta to be kidding me Claire." He rolled out of bed and went to the kitchen. The smell of bacon hit his nose as he stepped out of the bedroom as he turned into the kitchen Claire handed him his cup of coffee. He gave her a kiss and hugged her close to him and whispered, "Why are you up so early?" She replied, "I was too excited to stay sleep, so I got up to cook breakfast." His stomach let out a long loud moan and grumbles. She laughed and jokingly asked, "Gee you think it's hungry?" He chuckled and said, "Nah, I'm two quarts past starving; can ya help a brother out? What ya cooking?" Before she answered she went over to the oven and took out a pan of biscuits and a pan of bacon. Then she turned to say, "Biscuits, bacon, eggs and grits; just a little something, something to start the day." Before she finished her answer, Daniel had two biscuits in a plate pouring syrup over them. She didn't bother commenting on how greedy he looked eating them; wouldn't do any good he doesn't hear a word she be saying while eating biscuits. She took another plate and put the grits, eggs and bacon on it and sat it next to the other one. She fixed herself a small plate and sat down beside him to see he had three more biscuits and had eatin half the food in the plate she just put down. She had to say something, "Daniel slow down, that food ain't trying to run away from you; although it should." He just kept just kept devouring the food as she laughed at him. She loves to see him eat up the biscuits, he has always said, "Baby yo biscuits melt in yo mouth; you have to eat another one to taste the first one." He finished his second plate of biscuits when she said laughing, "Honey you ate like a pig, you should be ashamed of yourself but you're not." He laughed and said, "Yeah well that's what happens when ya come across some good biscuits," he said rubbing and patting his stomach. Her smile faded for a moment, she tried to hide it, but Daniel noticed and asked, "What's wrong babe? Was it something I said?" He pulled his chair closer to hug her; as a tear slides down her face she answers, "Yeah well all those years of me doing drugs you couldn't have known how good my biscuits were." He holds her tight and softly says, "Don't do this to yourself babe, that's the past." He tilts her head up, "Look at me Claire, God has forgiven you for that; it's time you forgive yourself and keep moving forward. I love the woman you are now. Just like you I have a second chance at being a better man, husband and father if God will permit it." She wiped her tears away and said, "You're right honey, God is so good to us; it's just that I get so nervous every time I think about us being parents again. I believe with all my heart God placed those children in our lives for a reason. I love them so much Daniel; I don't want to lose them." Daniel holds Claire hands and says, "You know Claire, when God does something, he does it right. When he says it's finished you better believe it is? Right now, he is working things out for us concerning the children, we don't have to do anything except wait and say thank you lord when it is done." "You know Daniel; I never thought I'd be so happy to have so many children loving me as their mom. We went from having one child, to no child, to ten. God sure does have some kind of sense of humor when he restores you of a loss." They started laughing about it as the children started entering the kitchen one by one. They all asked, "What's so funny?" Daniel and Claire both said, "God" Then started laughing again. The children were perplexed by the answer; they always thought of God being serious. They were quiet until Stacey came in talking about the holiday trip. Daniel and Claire were taken by surprise and were speechless to hear each child express their love for them. They didn't know the children thought so highly of them; they were only thinking of their love for the children. They forgot to ask the children how they felt, but now they know. Finally, Claire found the words to say, "Time to move forward."

Going back to school after a holiday break meant turning brain on to start the learning all over again. The children were more chatty than normal; everybody had a story to tell about their holiday and the relatives that visited. The block party was the icing on the cake of the conversation until Eddy and Red man told why they weren't there; then there were all kinds of Island questions. They talked about the beaches, shopping and the big boat ride. Everybody laughed at how Jamar and Red man got them sent home early; but they told how the boat ride ended early not how they ended up being sent home to be alone. Pretending to be functioning as a normal family was beginning to frustrate them. Shannon was relieved she didn't have to pretend anymore; everybody in the hood knew what her dad did to her, and they were looking out for her. They all put the Ms. Belinda incident behind them and concentrated more on protecting their leader. The Delray gang did not put it behind them, and they were coming to make her pay. One of the older girls told her cousin Shane in Delray about it not knowing that he was a gang member. She couldn't read a lick; but Shannon took out the time to help her. To her cousin that meant he owed Shannon for teaching his favorite cousin how to read. She has no brother; he was all she had for protection until Shannon came along and united the gangs in Boynton. His payment to Shannon is revenge for what Ms. Belinda did to her; he's been sneaking around campus casing the place to implement his plan. A few kids noticed the stranger coming around but by the time they reported someone being on campus he was gone. He made sure he was not seen by many; he would disappear before they could report he was there. He got familiar with the campus to find his way around enough to blend in with the older kids as they would be changing classes. He hung around long enough to get familiar with Belinda's routine around campus. He wasn't expecting her to be so young and attractive; she carried herself like she knew it too. A few of the guys in the gang have warrants for crimes they committed in Boynton Beach; Shane was one of them. What he plans to do to Belinda will have to be done quickly; he does not intend to get caught. He makes it off campus once again during a class exchange without being seen; the next time he returns he will not be alone. Shannon's phobias have gotten worse; she's washing her hands more and more each day. Her reason for doing it is everything has germs; she feels dirty every time she touches something. When she eats, she goes and brushes her teeth or makes a loud annoying sound sucking the food from between her gums. Every now and then it irritates everybody so to the point that they all yells at her to stop. When they ask her why she does it; she simply says her teeth are dirty. They looked at her strange at first until some of them ran their tongue across their teeth and realized theirs were dirty too; so, they stopped bothering her about it and ignored her. But not Sasha; she notices and remembers everything. She knows why it all started; and she tells Shannon every day, "You are clean now; I made sure I washed it off you. Please, you have to forget." Shannon always tells Sasha, "I don't know how to forget Sasha; I'm broken like humpty dumpty, I can't be fixed. She didn't know how to describe what happened in her mind. The voices kept repeating over and over; you're dirty. Washing her hands seemed to make them stop. Being in Ms. Belinda's class knowing she didn't like her wasn't easy. Eddy made her feel better by telling her what it was like having parents that didn't love them. Eddy told Shannon about Daniel and Claire because she knew she could trust her not to tell anyone else. Shannon goes over to Claire's to talk about her problems. Claire is trying to teach her how to use God's love to forgive; but Shannon needs love and is clueless on how to give it. She gives good advice to Eddy in telling her to love Claire and be glad God put them in her life. Sadly, she says to Eddy, "I pray God will send me new parents; I hate the ones I got." She started daydreaming about what her life would be like with new parents. She started telling Sasha her daydreams as a bedtime story to get her to go to sleep. Shannon didn't tell Wanda about Eddy's family because she knew Joyce was seeing Eddy's dad; that information came from Sasha who saw them kissing in the graveyard. She didn't believe Sasha at first until Sasha took her there to see for herself; but it was more than kissing going on. She had to tell Sasha to never tell anyone what they saw it's their big secret. Sasha loves keeping secrets; it makes her feel like a big girl with responsibilities.

At school all the children are excited there are only a few days left then Christmas break begins. They've been so busy going to Christmas plays and planning parties no one noticed Shane and his gang coming on campus. Shannon was not as excited as the others; she plans to ask Barbara if she could be taken out of Ms. Belinda's class after the holidays. She is not comfortable there anymore; she wants a fresh start for the New Year. The bell rings for them to change class, Shannon, Eddy and Wanda heads downstairs to science class. Miss Belinda is walking a head of them on her way to the main office as she normally does this time of day. She is almost at the bottom as Shannon takes a step down at the top; all of a sudden two guys grabs her and drags her down the rest of the stairs. They hit her in her mouth before she could scream for help. Shannon started running down the stairs to yell at them to stop; but somebody fired off a gun as three shots ring out in the air. Shannon saw them pull Miss Belinda towards the bathrooms then chaos struck. No one heard her scream, "HELP! Miss Belinda is in trouble!" Everyone was screaming and running for their lives and tripping over each other. Shannon had to hug the rails to keep from falling; she then realized she had to find Sasha.

CHAPTER FOUR

Sasha and Mrs. Vinegar were getting along better since Barbara came to the school. The children at Sasha's table were reading better now that Mrs. Vinegar is teaching the whole class. No one was peeing in class thanks to Sasha again. They had apple juice with their lunch which meant most of them had to go to the bathroom. Sasha finally had to go as it was almost time for class to end; she had ten minutes. She ran towards the end of the hall as fast as she could go; but quickly stopped when she saw a group of guys hiding under the stairs and between cars. She wanted to turn around and go back and tell the teacher about the strangers, but she really had to go; so, she decided to use the bathroom first. She made a mad dash in to use the first stall she could get to doing the pee-pee dance. The other girls washed up and ran out to get back to class before the bell rang. The bell rang before she could finish; not long after she thought she heard someone scream but was scared by the sound of three loud bang, bang, and bang. She quickly jumped off the toilet and pulled up her panties crooked and half rolled up. Before she could come out of the stall, she heard other people in the bathroom with her. She quietly climbed back on the toilet; the sounds they were making did not sound safe at all. She stepped towards the back of the toilet to peep through the crack of the divider. Two men were beating a lady who was trying to get away from them. Belinda screamed as they grabbed her again and threw her on the floor. Before they could hit her again Sasha flushed the toilet by mistake; she was so scared all she could do was say, "Please sirs, don't hit her again; you're hurting her." Shane motioned the other guy to put Belinda in one of the stalls as he called for Sasha to come out. "Come on out little one, I won't hurt ya. What's your name?" Trembling she answered, "Sasha" as tears started flowing down her face. Then she said, "My big sister is Shannon and she is going hurt you if you hurt me." Shane kneeled down to Sasha and said, "Listen little one;

what she's getting done to her is payback for what she did to Shannon. You have to go little girl; you can't see this." He walked her to the door. Sasha leaned against the wall looked up while crying said, "But it's wrong to do that." He said to her, "Pay back baby girl," then turned and went back in the bathroom. Sasha was really scared for Miss Belinda she didn't know what else to do except cry. The hallway was filled with people running and screaming all around Sasha as she leaned against the wall still crying. Shannon made it downstairs and was surprised to see Sasha outside the bathroom leaning on the wall. There was no time to ask questions she just scooped her up in her arms and ran like their lives depended on it. The gang burst a few windows out but as soon as Shane came out the bathroom, they all ran off campus mingling in with the older kids. Some children were trampled by the crowds and were badly bruised with broken bones. No one knew what to do or where to go for safety. The police with swat teams and other law enforcement agencies surrounded the school but the gang was long gone by then. Shannon, Eddy and Wanda ran all the way home not looking back to see if any of the others made it out. Children were crying and hiding in places they were too afraid to come out of. No one was shot; the gun was fired to cause chaos so Shane could get to Belinda without being noticed. Law enforcement officers managed to get everyone calmed down so the injured could be treated. Emergency tents were set up on the grassy areas of campus to treat the broken legs, arms and those with slight concussions. Counselors were sent in to assess the emotional trauma the children sustained. Nothing prepared them for what they saw when Belinda came crawling out of the bathroom. What they did to her was horrifying; no one recognized the badly beaten body crawling on the sidewalk, there was an eerie silence for three seconds. First responders rushed to her aide to find that she had been raped and beaten to a pulp; she could only moan as she try to cry out for help, it was a miracle she survived. Mr. Bailey recognized her and ran over to her crying out her name; what he saw made him sick to his stomach. Her face was swollen from a broken jaw, she had a broken collar bone and two broken ribs; her life had been shattered. Principal Bailey was in tears and was so angry by what he saw; he began to ask himself, who could be so cold to do this to someone just before the holidays? Why? Why would they do this? He then realized that Belinda was the only one on campus that was attacked. Then he began to blame himself for not listening to the children when they told him a stranger came on campus. I know I appointed someone to keep a look out for strangers (he thought). Did they look; or did they just said they looked and didn't. I should've done more, but how could I have known this was going to happen. He looked over at the ambulance taking Belinda to the hospital and said out loud, "Live Belinda, please fight to live." They were questioning all the children to see if anyone remembers seeing anyone out of the ordinary. The only person who could describe the strangers was not there. Sasha cried the rest of the day because she couldn't get the image of Miss Belinda being beat out of her mind. She couldn't think to describe what happened; she'd been traumatized by the violence. First Shannon and now Belinda, it was too much for her to process and make sense of it all. She wanted to tell Shannon the man did it for her, but she couldn't get the words to come out. Shannon knew something was terribly wrong with her baby sister the moment she asked what was wrong. Sasha just stood there trembling and crying; Shannon picked her up and took her to the bathroom to give her a bath. She looked at Sasha and realized she must have seen something very bad then thought; I know I got her away from there as fast as I could. She didn't know how to get Sasha to talk about it; it occurred to her to take Sasha to Mrs. Claire. Before she could get Sasha dressed, she had already left the bathroom and went to bed. Shannon looked in on her and decided to let her sleep; she held Sasha's small hand in hers and said, "Poor thing you've been through a lot today." She stepped out the back door and headed over to Wanda's house. Gwen ran up to her and asked, "Did you hear what happened to Miss Belinda? Shannon stopped abruptly and put both hands over her mouth as she remembered seeing two guys snatch Belinda towards the bathroom. Looking at Gwen with a fearful stare she answered, "No, what happened to her?" Gwen couldn't wait to spread the juicy news; she figured Shannon would be eager to hear about it considering the fact that Belinda had bad vibes toward her. She smiled then said, "Giirrll somebody beat the crap out of her; it was so bad nobody recognized her. She ain't pretty Miss Pussy lips now, hahaha." Shannon turned and looked back at the house thinking of where she picked Sasha up at school. She asked without looking at Gwen, "Where was she attacked?" Gwen excitedly answered not noticing Shannon acting strange, "In the girl's bathroom; they say she crawled out naked, bloody and broke up. Girl she was looking a hot mess. They said Principle Bailey broke down and cried gator tears when he recognized who she was." Before Gwen could finish Shannon ran back to the house; she realized Sasha was already crying when she picked her up outside the bathroom. She started crying as she figured out what was wrong with Sasha; she saw it and she knows who did it. A wave of fear came over her as she realizes Sasha is the only one who could identify Belinda's attackers. Shannon stood there frozen with fear looking at her baby sister sleeping peacefully. All she could say was, "Oh my God, oh my God; your sweet little angel if that's what you saw it's too much for you to say." Gwen came in the door, Girl what happened to you? You left me standing in the street talking to myself." She quickly lowered her voice when she saw Sasha was sleep, "Oops, sorry." Shannon wiped tears away and said, "Sorry, I forgot I left Sasha in the tub bathing by herself; but it looks like she's okay." She pushed Gwen out the door to go back to

Wanda's house; she dare not tell her Sasha seen the whole thing and who did it. Then again, she's really not sure what all Sasha saw. Gwen finished telling Shannon how Belinda looked finally ending the tale with, "It's a miracle she's still alive." They got to Wanda's house only to discover everybody else was coming over talking about Miss Belinda and why she was the only one attacked. As they all gave their opinion as to why it happened; Shannon realized Sasha is the key to solving this mystery, but she's not talking. In a way it's good because no one needs to know that a six-year-old witnessed that yet. Gwen said to Shannon, "Girl you should be glad Belinda got what was coming to her for what she did to you, pay back is a mother…" Everybody replied at the same time, "Gwen that was mean of you to say that; you have no mercy." Eddy said, "I wouldn't wish that on my worst enemy." Wanda gave Gwen a nudge on her shoulder and said, "Gwen how could you be so cruel and say that? What happened to Miss Belinda has changed her life forever. Whoever did it was a heartless person." They sat in silence for a moment no one had anything else to say. Shannon wasn't talking because she was about to cry; she knows what Belinda will be going through once she's healed. The pain will be gone from the outside, but the inside will be in pain for a long time; it may never heal. Tears began to well up in her eyes, but she got up and went to the bathroom; it's the one place you can go and sit to cry in silence without being disturbed. She sat and wept a moment to get herself together. Then a knock on the door followed by a sweet little voice asking, "Who's in there? I got to use the toilet. She stood up and flushed so it would seem like she was actually using it; she washed her hands opened the door to see little Triqua doing the pee-pee dance. Shannon smiled and stepped out of the way as Triqua swished passed her. Well a bathroom isn't a quiet place to sit with a house full of kids. She joined the others just as Joyce entered to tell them there's no school the rest of the week Christmas break is starting early; however, there will be counselors coming around to talk to everybody about the shooting.

Kenny called The Department of Children and Family Services a week after they got home. He reported that their parents had abandoned them. He was tired of his part time parents as he called them. He's tired of being a parent; right now, he feels they need full time parents. He did not tell Daniel or the other kids what he did. No one came to investigate at first and he was starting to worry. He started making them stay at the house. After the school shooting it kind of put a sense of urgency for D.C.F to visit them at home. They mainly want to see if any of the kids need counseling since the shooting at school. The case worker came to the house while Eddy was over to Joyce house with Wanda and Shannon. Kenny let the utilities get shut off to make sure they would be taken into custody. The windows and doors were left opened all the time to allow air and light in.

The lady asked to talk to their parents, Kenny didn't hesitate to answer, "They're not here, and they hardly are now days." The case worker asked, "What do you mean not here? Have they stepped out for a moment to come back? Or are they gone for good not here? Kenny was looking mean as ever to try and show that he really didn't want the lady prying. Stacey didn't know what to make of his attitude, so she answered speaking soft and sweet, "We saw them just before Thanksgiving, and we even had a big meal with them; but haven't seen them since. We didn't know that would be our last meal." Kenny nudged her with his elbow tilting his head towards the door. She stepped back and said, "Excuse me ma'am I have to get someone;" she ran out of the house. Eddy Gal was on her way home unaware of the unexpected visitor at the house. Stacey met her in the middle of the street filling her in on what was going on before they got in the house. The case worker was walking around the house checking out its condition while talking on the phone. She acted like everything was the usual until she came in a room and saw baby Queen sleeping on a pile of clothes for a bed. Whoever she was talking to on the phone was getting yelled at. "I need law enforcement here now! I don't care which one just get them here now with a van; this is unacceptable!" she somehow managed to fake a smile when she turned around to see nine kids grouped together staring at her. She calmly said to them, "It's okay kids we're working on getting you some help and we're going to work on locating your parents. Do they ever tell you guys where they are going?" All the children answered, "No ma'am, they just leave us." Her phone rings and she answer it just as a van and two police cars pulls in front of the house. The children hug each other and begin crying as they see policemen come in the door. As soon as she says to them, "You're going to be alright now children;" the screaming started. She asked Kenny if they knew of any relatives that live nearby that they could go to and stay with until their parents are located. Kenny almost leaped for joy, but he kept his composer. She asked the right question he was hoping she would. He answered trying his best to sound afraid, "No ma'am, but we do have a guardian in case of an emergency. The lady was shocked by his answer, "Really? So why haven't you contacted them when your parents leave you?" Kenny held his head down as if he was ashamed and said, "Well we didn't think it was an emergency yet ma'am, I'm sorry." She walked over to him and lifts his head up with her finger under his chin to say, "Son you didn't know that you were in a state emergency after three days; you just trying to survive. Now tell me who your guardian is so we could leave you with them until we locate your parents." The screaming and crying stopped once they realized what Kenny had done to them. She gathered them together and had Kenny and Stacey pack clothes and toys to take with them. Two officers walked them to the van to load them in. Stacey was surprised not to see hardly any of their new clothes in the house. She asked Kenny, "What happened to all our new clothes mom bought us?" Kenny looked at her and smiled then said, I broke into that new house and hid them in the storage area under the stairs. We'll get them later when we find out where we're staying." They both laughed at how everything was starting go like they wanted it. Stacey said to him, "Next time let me in on what you're doing; you had me scared for real." Kenny said to her, "If I had done that you wouldn't have been as scared as the others. I needed everybody being surprised, scared and the tears; all of it had to be real in order for this to work out. We get to see the surprise on Daniel and Claire's face when we show up at their door with a D.C.F case worker and two policemen; they don't know what I've done either. This has to work because we are going to be home with them for good." They gathered all the bags and headed to the van. Kenny gave the case worker Daniel's address; she got in her car and led the van and one police car two streets over. They pulled up just as Claire was coming out of the house carrying a big box and sitting next to other boxes in the yard. The case worker gets out and walks over to talk to Claire who by now is scared out her wits seeing the children in a police van pull up to the house. The case worker asks, "Is this the residence of Daniel and Claire Hubbs?" Claire nervously answers, "Yes I am…uh…I mean it is how can I help you?" The lady looks up from flipping through papers on a clipboard, "I'm sorry Mrs. Hubbs my name is Vickie, I'm with the Department of Children and Family Services. The children say that you and your husband Daniel Hubbs are their guardians; is that correct?" "Yes, it is," Claire answers as her heart starts beating fast and hard. Would you show me the papers verifying that if you don't mind; I need to make sure the children are in a safe place until we can locate their parents." Claire didn't know what to think at first, "Ahh yes, the papers; please follow me it's in the new house. We are in process of moving in our new house; it got finished earlier than we anticipated." They walked across the street Vickie was impressed with the big house. When she pulled up to the little house, she was thinking there was no way ten kids were going to fit in there; she wasn't going to allow it. Claire called out to Daniel as he was upstairs putting beds together. Furniture was delivered early that morning; he was glad to take a break. He quickly ran down but abruptly stopped when he saw a strange lady standing beside his wife. "Umm, hello?" He said not sure if she was there for good or bad news. As she stepped forward to introduce herself Claire went in the office to get the papers. "Hi, my name is Vickie I'm with D.C.F; your wife is getting proof of guardianship of the children." Before she could explain any further Claire came back, "Got it right here!" She hands Vickie the papers; she gives it a quick look over hands it back to Claire and says, "Everything looks to be in order; we'll be contacting you when the parents have or have not been located. A counselor will be by to evaluate the emotional state the children are in; I will document in our records that the children are in your care temporarily thank you for your time Mr. and Mrs. Hubbs have a good day." Vickie signaled the police to let the children out of the van and unload their clothes. She made a phone call as the officers got the kids out; got in her car and they all left. Claire looked up at her husband and asked, "Daniel is this really happening? God moves in mysterious ways." They stood there hugging each other and praising God. The children ran in the house cheering and jumping up and down excited to finally be a family with Daniel and Claire. The little ones Candice and Neil ran to Kenny hugged both his legs and said, "We love your big brother". They all hugged Daniel and Claire who is still shocked that they actually have the children to love as their own. Daniel immediately started thinking about how he was going to tell the guys about it at the next meeting. The plan is going to have to be pushed forward with urgency; the children's impatience may have jeopardized their lives. As soon as D.C.F contacts Romeo to inform him they have their kids there will be hell to pay. Daniel knows he will have to kill him if he comes anywhere near his family. The children are so happy now; but he knows their moment of happiness is his and Claire's nightmare.

Joyce was bringing the girls something to drink when Stacey came over and literally drug Eddy Gal out the street with no explanation. She didn't think much of it until a police cruiser and van pulled up to the house across the street. Fifteen minutes later she heard the children screaming and crying; Joyce and the other kids walked to the edge of the driveway to witness the chaos. Stanley's limo slowly came up then briefly stopped as Stan rolled down his window to exchange a few words with the officers; his limo proceeded to slowly pull away. That made Joyce wonder why he was being so nosey. Are the children being taken away from their parents? The cops went in the house then came out with baby Queen and the other two little ones and put them in the van. When she saw the D.C.F case worker come out she realized she was there asking about the school shooting. Poor kids your parents aren't around to rescue you, she thought to herself. She talked to Vickie earlier she recalled then mumbled, "I guess she finally made it over there." Wanda and Shannon stood next to her sadly watching their friend crying getting in the van. Finally, they asked, "What's going to happen to them?" Joyce jumped slightly startled at the fact the girls was standing so close; she didn't know they came out with her. She answered, "Oh they'll be placed in foster homes for a little while until their parents come get them. I hope they keep them all together though." Both girls sadly said at the same time, "Me too." The three of them stood there watching the cars and van pulls away and disappears down the street. They turned to go back in the house when Shannon suddenly stopped and said, "Oh no, I got to go check on Sasha!" She quickly ran home through the wooded path in back of the house with Wanda closely behind her. Joyce slowly makes her way back in the house; fear overcame her as she thinks about how pissed Romeo is going to be when he finds out. She spoke out loud and said, "Somebody's going to have hell to pay for that." She didn't know Greg was in the room until he asked, "Hell to pay for what?" She jumps and squeaks out, "Maaann, don't scare me like that!" He laughed and said, "Hey, I was just sitting here; hell, to pay for what? She sat down and said, "The state just took Jerome and Kate's kids." Greg looks out the window and says, "Huh did they now? Well things are moving faster than expected. I better call the fellas together to meet and see where we go from here." But before he could make the call his phone rings; Stan calls to let him know what took place across the street and where the children are going. He hangs up and began to walk towards the door, but Joyce stops him and ask, "Why aren't you telling me about what's going on in the meetings? He turned around and looked at her with a serious frown and said, "You pushed one button too many the last time and we are not going to have this conversation again." He went out the door and walked to Stan's house. To have the most privacy they all met at Stanley's house; as they all settled down Daniel stood up to make an announcement. "Ahh, fellas first of all I have an explanation as to why we are meeting so soon like this. I'll make it short, so I won't waste anybody's time; Ahh my wife has been taking care of the children; they tricked their mom into signing a guardianship paper. We had it notarized by a friend who owed me one. The shooting happened at school and now I have temporary custody of the children which is why we are here." He quickly sits down to brace himself for questions. The room is quiet for five minutes as some of the guys are trying to figure out what was said. Bryan was first to speak, "Man what the hell you talkin bout? And whose children you got? What the fuck that's gotta do with us?" Stanley stood up and said, "Daniel that is the worst explanation I have ever heard about a serious situation man; you dropped the ball on that one. Guys what Daniel was trying to tell us is that he has custody of Jerome's children. His wife has been taking care of them for quite some time, which means he's in some serious shit when Jerome finds out. The children put things in motion faster than what we wanted; so, we need to catch up and act fast what's done is done." Skip stood up and walked over to Daniel and gave him a fist pump with a handshake then said, "Don't worry about its man, I gotcha back. When he gets back in town, I'll be on him like white on rice watching every move he makes." Greg notice Skip really hates Jerome like he has a personal vendetta to settle with him; he calmly tells him, "Skip man, keep it calm we can't show our hand on what we plan to do to him. Stay on the down low with this man." Stanley continues to talk and says, "I agree this is Vegas guys; what goes on in here stays here." He goes over to his safe and pulls out some papers and shares the contents with them. "Now here's what we got to do when he comes back home; Skip since you insist on keeping an eye on him you notify D.C.F. They may or may not let him know who has the kids but if they tell him Skip you're going to have to move in on him fast; get him to us as soon as you get the jump on him." The meeting was over as every man had a part to play in the ending of Jerome's life; but when it comes to planning a murder thing don't always go as you plan. These good Samaritans will soon find that out.

How delighted was the children to learn the house was being built for them? It was even funnier when he told Daniel he hid their new clothes in the storage under the stairs. Daniel was wise to save most of his money while driving trucks; he spent some of his time away from home doing extra runs to get away from a drug addicted wife delivering drugs for some big-time drug dealers. He didn't care where the extra money came from at that time, he needed it to get away for good; at least that's what he was planning. His last run would have gotten him Fed time in prison if Tate hadn't killed himself; his son's death spared him lock up time. Another driver picked up the shipment for him and got caught; when he found out it gave him a good reason to go to church with his wife and get some Jesus. Now he may be about to lose his life saving somebody's children they don't want; but it's worth it. He sometimes wished someone would've been there to save Tate's life because he wasn't. He didn't tell Claire or the children about the danger they face being a family; he just wanted to enjoy every moment he has with them. A new house and a second chance at being a better husband and father; can't ask for a better Christmas than this Daniel thought to himself.

James and Barbara actually went out and got the kids really nice toys for Christmas. Although Barbara loved the holidays, she still was not trusting James being around Shannon alone. Shannon's phobias were starting to get the best of her since hearing about what happened to Miss Belinda. Everything needed to be cleaned because it has germs; and germs makes everything dirty. She taught Sasha how to clean away germs from everything she touch; it's how she got her to talk about what she saw in the bathroom at school with Claire's help, but she made Sasha promise not to tell anyone else. Shannon met with David and told him what the Delray gang did at the school and why. David told her why their actions bothered her so much; but he has to respect the brotherhood code when it comes to avenging the honor of someone special to the hood as her. Shannon forgot how special she was outside her home; David reminded her that she was a gang leader herself. David knew Shane's gang very well; they use to do drug runs together. David never liked Shane's method of doing things they were too violent that's why he stopped hanging with them. He knew he had to thank Shane for honoring Shannon even if the method was wrong, he had to be discreet with the meeting. D.C.F got to Shannon and Sasha after Claire talked with them and prayed for them. Now Sasha was all about

Jesus making everything better for her. She talked with Vickie and told her she is better now that Jesus dried all her tears and took away her fears. Shannon wouldn't let Sasha tell everything she saw she interrupted to say, "After we heard the shots, I picked up my little sister and ran home. I didn't know about what happened to Miss Belinda until the next day. Is she okay? Does she have someone to look after her? Vickie looks at Shannon to say, "Yes, her parents came to take care of her; its sweet of you to ask." She saw how sincere Shannon was when asking about Belinda. Then Shannon asked, "Will she be coming back when school start again? Vickie answered, "I'm afraid that won't be possible she was hurt really bad to come back so soon; but keep her in your prayers." Vickie left after being satisfied with children's wellbeing. Twenty minutes later Shannon wished she'd told her about what happened to her maybe she would be on her way to a good family like Eddy Gal.

Greg and Joyce were sitting in the den enjoying a quiet moment together with no kids. Greg's parents came and got the kids and took them to Orlando to Disney World. The day after Christmas Greg will be leaving to close a very important business deal. He hopes to be back before New Year's but wasn't sure. As he is packing Joyce looks at him with love in her eyes and says, "You know you're leaving me all alone with so much free time; what am I to do without you?" He gives her a tender kiss on the lips and says, "You shop till you drop." They both laugh and hug each other close as if for the last time. She wanted to ask him about the last meeting they had but instead said, "Well if you're not back by New Year's I will not celebrate it without you." Thinking, I hope Romeo gets back so I can warn him. He kisses her on the forehead and says, "I tell you what let's throw a New Year's party when I get back home. We need to restock the bar it's still very low from Thanksgiving." She looks up at him and says, "Let's go do that now while you are here with me because I am not getting all that liquor by myself." He finished packing then they left to go to the liquor store. They got back stocked the bar then decided to shower and go to bed early but not to sleep. They made love for a long time as Joyce realized why she married Greg and why they had so many children. He puts so much passion into loving her she never wants him to stop. The fore play alone makes her toes curls, although he's a very strong man his hands gently caresses along her body from head to her toes. There's no pain here she thinks, just sheer pleasure. Her moans, groans and deep inhales and exhales let him know he is doing everything right. She just wanted to melt away in his arms. She moaned out the words, "I love you so much babe." At that moment she decided she didn't need anyone else but her husband; bump warning Romeo she's just going to tell him it's over and start the New Year out being faithful to her man. Morning came fast for the two love birds as they were up enjoying breakfast together catering to each other needs like newlyweds on honeymoon. They spent the next two days decorating the house for the Christmas party which they didn't go all out with it since the children wasn't there. They spent more of their time loving each other since Greg had to leave early to keep a client from leaving the company. She drove him to the airport to see him off; they stood near the gate of his of his departure hugging and kissing like a couple falling in love for the first time. They were even making plans to continue the romance the time they are together. Greg departed not knowing that this would be the last moment of romance they would have with each other.

The Christmas party went well for everybody, but Joyce was missing Greg. Stanley invited everybody over to his place to bring the New Year in. The information he had on Jerome and Kathryn was turned over to the state for D.C.F to investigate. He decides it was time to bring the New Year in with a bang; so, he arranged for fireworks to be held at his house, his way of thanking them for making him apart of their families. Joyce was home on the phone with Greg as he was telling her he would not be home for New Year's Day, but he will be home two days later. At first, she didn't want to go to the party, but all the ladies stopped by and made her get out the house. The guys had a quick meeting as Stanley gave them an update on Jerome's happy life about to turn sour. "Be on the lookout for them coming back soon Skip." Stanley had rooms prep for families to stay over rather than go home drunk and not make it. There were two large rooms to hang out in: one for the drinkers and the other for no drinkers. Both rooms were crowded and noisy; before Joyce started drinking, she decided to go home and get an overnight bag to spend the night. Just as she was leaving the house phone rings; she looked and saw it was Jerome then decided not to answer and walked out the door. As midnight approached the drunks decide to join the sober people to bring in the New Year together; Joyce got back in time to grab a glass of champagne and toast to new beginnings.

The weather was beautiful this time of the year on the Island; no bad storms Kate thought to herself as she walked along the beach. She was on her way back in the house when she heard Jerome yelling out to her, "How the hell did D.C.F get the number here? What the fuck is going on?" Kate looking confused asked, what do you mean D.C.F? What are you talking about? He backed down his anger and thought about his response. "I just got a call from the authorities here saying D.C.F in the U.S want us to meet with them concerning our children. They wouldn't tell me what was going on with them." Kate's heart skipped a beat as fear took over her as she suspected the children maybe in D.C.F custody and they will be going to jail for abandonment. Romeo was mad they found out where they were; Kate finally said to him, "Shut up, they have our kid's you idiot. They want us home to face child abandonment charges. I'm just like my parents; I've just fucked up my children's life." She began crying saying, "How did I let it get like this? Why is this happening now?" Romeo walked over to her and hugged her to say, "It's going to be okay; I'm going to call a friend and find out if they know where the kids are you get us a good lawyer. What a way to bring in the New Year." He tried calling Joyce every hour getting mad each time she didn't pick up. All kinds of thoughts started running through his head; like somebody wants them locked up or they're jealous of his and Kate's lifestyle. By the time he made the last call to Joyce he convinced himself she turned them in. "I know she's jealous because I've been spending time with Kate and not her." He mumbled out loud to himself. His temper started fuming out of control as he spoke out loud, "I'm going to kill that bitch when I do get back; that'll teach her to fuck up my life." He didn't care about New Year's celebrations he just figured Joyce is supposed to be at his beckoning call. They got a pilot to fly them back to Florida the next day on their private jet. Jerome wants to deal with Joyce first before he meets with D.C.F to answer for the children. Kathryn was torn with regrets of not being a good mother to her children and now they are gone. She knows she has been worse with them than her parents have been to her. Her parents left her in a safe environment and made sure she was well cared for. There is no way I would survive in jail she thought; but she spoke out saying, "I'd rather die than go in that place." She looked over at Jerome and noticed him fuming in anger about not contacting his so-called friend; probably one of his whores who wasn't available at his beckon call. She smiled as she assured herself that if anything happened to her he would not get one cent of her wealth. She then began thinking of ways to end her life because nothing else mattered now that the children are gone. Finally, the plane lands in Florida and a limo is there to take them home; of course, Doug is the driver he called Skip to let him they were back in the State. Doug drops them off at the house turns around to go park the limo around the corner to meet skip. It's early in the morning as they arrive to walk in a house with no lights, no water and no kids. The neighborhood is quiet as everybody is still sleeping off the late celebration at Stanley house except Skip; his house is next door to Romeo's he walks in his back door after meeting with Doug. He went in his office to sit in the dark and look out the side window and wait. With Greg not being home he knows there's going to be a meeting between Joyce and Jerome, and he intends to be there when it happens. As far as Skip was concerned, he's going to make sure it's Romeo's last meeting with Joyce. He's not going to make it to the hotel with her this time. Skip arranged for some hookers to lead Jerome down a certain alley where he'll be waiting; the hookers were more than happy to help. None of the ladies like Romeo after he almost killed two of them; they wanted revenge any way they could get it.

Joyce called Barbara to see if she wanted to go out to the club with her before her kids come back home. Barb said yes and was all excited about going out with her friend. Shannon was happy to be going over to spend the night with Wanda; but just as they were getting ready to go out the back-door Sasha said to her, "I don't feel good." She started sweating then passed out. Shannon ran to Barb yelling, "Sasha is very sick mom she passed out!" Luckily Gwen's mom was just passing by when she heard Shannon yell out. She rushed in to see if she could help; she's a nurse at the hospital. She ran over to see Sasha on the floor. She checked to see if there was a pulse and found that Sasha had a high fever. She picked her up and told Barb and Shannon to come with her to the hospital. Barb wasn't thinking about going to the club as she was holding her limp hot baby in her arms. Tears started flowing down her face as the thought of losing another child entered her mind. Shannon is crying in the back thinking this is not the right time to lose her baby sister; she starts praying, "God if you can hear me please don't take my sister away. I know I always say she gets on my nerves, but I love her. She is the only one who keeps me stable besides you. Please God if you can let me keep her. Shirley brought the car to a screeching halt in front of the emergency door and ran in to get help. Barb was right behind her with Sasha dangling in her arms. They directed her to a room to lay her on the bed as doctors and nurses surrounded her yelling out medical commands as instruments were being wheeled in from every direction. Barb could no longer see her baby girl from so many people being in the room around the bed; by the time they cleared out Sasha's tiny body had tubes coming from every angle seems like. Barb slowly approached the tiny lifeless body not knowing what to think of the tubes and the machines; every machine had its own sound. Shirley came in with Shannon to let her know they were running tests and the doctor will be with her soon to let her know the results. An hour later the doctor comes in as Barb is sitting on the bed holding the one free hand on her daughter's body. He introduces himself then started asking questions, "Mrs. Kingsley has the child been around anyone sick that you know of? Or has she picked up any dead birds? Come in contact with pigeons that you know of?" Barb answered, "I don't know I'm not sure if any of her friends were sick." The doctor said sympathetically, "Well Mrs. Kingsley there's no good news I have to tell you; your daughter has Rubella its German measles which are very deadly and frankly we don't know if she's going to make it. Many kids die from this all we can do is fight the fever and pray she pulls through with no brain damage." As the doctor turns to leave James and

Robert is standing in the door listening to the bad news. Robert tells James, "I think you should wait to tell her about her friend man.

Joyce pulls up to Barbs house and blows the horn, but no one comes out. She gets out and go knock on the door, but no one answers that either; so, she decided to go to the bar without her friend figuring something may have come up and she will see her there later. She was unaware she was being followed by two people; Romeo was in a different car he didn't let her know he was back, and Skip was hot on his tail. Joyce parked in a space close to the club but just out from the alley where Skip parks on the other side where a pile of trash and the dumpster hide his car from view. Jerome waits for her to go inside so he pulls his car in the alley and parks behind the dumpster not far from Skip. Skip can't believe how easy Romeo just made it for him; now if the ladies get it right everything will go as planned. When the ladies saw Joyce comes into the club, they knew they would not be able to pull Romeo away from her. They had to figure out a way to get Joyce out before he comes; but before they could do that Romeo walks in. They all spread out and sat in different places watching Joyce as he spots her sitting alone at a table. He walks over to the table sat down and wasted no time letting her know how furious he was with her. He grabs her by the wrist tight and asked, "Woman why the hell you haven't been answering your phone?" He growled out loud; he was squeezing her wrist so tight the circulation was starting to go out of her fingers. Ouch! She yelled, "Let go of me you bastard!" She managed to snatch her wrist out of grip then got up and walked over to the bar. She asked the bartender for a drink; just as he gives it to her Romeo comes over and grabs her again. The bartender warns him, "Yo man, don't start that shit with the lady in here; not in my bar." Romeo glared at the bartender leaned on the counter towards him and growled out, "You better leave me the hell alone, and you don't know who you fuckin with boy." The bartender reached down and pulled up his shot gun and pointed it in Romeo's face and said, "Oh yes hell I do now back off!" Romeo quickly backed away with both hands up saying, "Okay cool its man, alright cool it." He turned and saw Joyce heading out the door and quickly followed; the other ladies grabbed their bats and followed him. He caught up with Joyce at her car pressing against the door preventing her from getting in. "Bitch why you sent D.C.F at me and my wife like that?" Joyce stepped away from him for the first time fearing for her life. She knew she was in danger, so she answered him as she was looking for a way to run. "There was a shooting at school that made D.C.F visit every house checking on all the kids. She tried to run down the alley, but he grabs her. He yells, "Liar!"

as he pulls her close to him, he grabs her head and twists it hard to the left and it snaps. Her body goes limp and falls to the pavement; he realizes he just killed the one person he loved. Before he could bend down to hold her in his arms ladies are running towards him screaming with bats and pipes in their hands. He panics and pushes Joyce body under her car then runs down the alley towards his car. Skip is kneeling between two dumpsters out of sight when he heard screams coming from entrance of the alley. He steps out to see Joyce body falls to the pavement and Romeo running towards him as the ladies are chasing him. He yells out, "Nooo!" Romeo is almost to his car as Skip steps out and yell; he stops and looks behind him at the ladies coming at him with bats and pipes, then decides to go forward to face Skip one on one. He runs towards Skip at full speed thinking he could tackle Skip down; but just as he got close enough Skip pulls a pipe to strike him, but two stray dogs' runs out of the trash pile and go between Romeo legs. He trips over the dogs falling to the side his head slams into the dumpster and he falls to the pavement out cold. Skip stands over him with the pipe in hand expecting him to get up, but he didn't. Skip runs to the van and gets a blanket to wrap Romeo in. The ladies help him as they are crying about what happened to Joyce. Skip breaks down and starts crying with the ladies as they are in disbelief that Joyce is dead. Skip doesn't know how he's going to tell Greg his wife is dead. They make sure no evidence is left of Romeo being hurt in the alley; even though the dogs caused his accident something else is going to cause his death. After skip left the ladies gave him twenty minutes to get where he was going with Romeo. They went in the club and told the bartender to call the police because Romeo just killed Joyce. He couldn't believe what he just heard. "I should've just shot him instead of letting him go so he could kill a good woman like that; I knew I should've done more. Tears started flowing as the cops came in thinking the body was inside the bar. The ladies took them where Joyce body lay under her car. They were all crying feeling bad about not trying harder to get Joyce to go home. They told their story on how it all happened so fast; they chased him down the alley, but they lost sight of him because he was a fast runner. They weren't sure what direction he ran in; he was gone by the time they got to the entrance of the alley, but his car was still there locked. The cops tapped off the area to make sure no one else went in or out until the investigators come. Skip and the guys had already pulled Romeo out of the van and down in the middle of the track over the canal. Skip was still crying uncontrollably as he were telling them how Romeo killed Joyce and how the dogs caused him to hit his head. They looked at the gash and saw a huge knot had formed and there was a lot of blood. Doug said, "With that bump he won't be living too long." He was still out cold as they heard the train's horn not far from the canal. They all cleared the area and went to Stanley's house to wait. They calmed Skip down by assuring him there was nothing he could've done to keep her alive. James bellowed out, "She shouldn't have been there." Before anything else could be said they heard the train horn blowing loud and long and coming to a screeching halt. They got up and ran out the house to see if the train derailed or something.

The conductor was glad school was in after a summer of cursing children out for playing chicken with his train. It's been quiet for a while over the canal the water is beautiful at night when the moon is over it. He started to slow the train down as he approaches the canal but decided to stay at speed considering the kids are never around during the holidays. Just as he gets to the middle something pops up on the tracks; he could barely make out what it is because it's too low on the tracks until he was too close on it. "It's a man!" He blows the horn long and loud yelling, "Shiiittt!!"…. He sees the body fly off the track into the dark as he brings the train to a screeching halt. He radios dispatch to let them know he just hit a man on the tracks over the canal. He grabs his flashlight jumps out to see if he could spot where the body landed. It's late and too dark; he can't even describe what the guy looks like it happened so fast. The nerves in hands started shaking as the thought of him killing somebody began to sink in; he sat down on the side of the embankment looking down on the water. He said out loud, "I can't do this anymore I need to retire." He heard the sirens blare and saw the flashing lights approach the park he stood up and began walking towards them.

Kate finished cleaning the house hours ago but was pissed at the fact that Romeo left her to do it by herself; it was late, and he still hadn't come home. "Where the hell are you Jerome?" She asked as if he could answer her. "You better not be with one of your whores; cause when I catch ya I'm gonna kill ya." She flopped down on the sofa after looking out the window for the umpteenth time to see if his car was pulling up in the driveway. She had the curtains pulled open so she will know when he comes home. She sat there and thought about the children and said, "I can't do this by myself where are you Jerome? She began crying thinking about how many times and how many ways she could have stopped this from happening. I'm not going to jail for those kids she thought then drifted off to sleep. The sound of sirens going by the house woke her up. She slowly walked over to the window half asleep checking, still no car. She began to worry Jerome never stayed out all night. More police cars flew by her house they seemed to have stopped at the park. What could be going on down there this time of the morning she wondered? She decided to slip on her slippers and go find out. Before she could get to the end of the driveway a plain car with flashing lights pulls up to her; two men gets out and show their badge. The driver does the talking, "Hello, are you Mrs. Padgett?" Her heart start beating fast and hard thinking they were coming to arrest her; she hesitated but answered, "Yes I am, what this is about officer?" The man corrected her, "Detective actually ma'am, we're looking for your husband is he home?" She pulls her hair back and answered, "I'm looking for him too; what has he done now?" The detective tilts his head slightly to the side with a questionable look on his face seeing that Kate clearly has no idea where her husband is. He tries to find a nice way to tell her but decided to spit it out, "He's wanted for murder; if he shows up give us a call. He hands her a card, but she slowly takes it not believing what she just heard. They got in the car then pulled out and headed to the park to blend in with the other flashing lights. Kate no longer had the desire to go and see what was going on; she went back in the house and sat on the sofa. "He's not coming back." Tears began flowing down as she repeated again, "He's not coming back; you're gonna let me face this shit by myself aren't you Jerome? Well I'm going to fix you Romeo or whatever the hell your whores call you! She started yelling out like a crazy woman, "I'm not doing it you hear me! I'm not doing it! She started tossing what little stuff she had in the house all over the place messing up what she just cleaned. She ran in the room screaming out over and over "I'm not doing it! She grabbed her purse and pulls out a bottle of pain pills she would take every now and then. A gift from Jerome when he beat her so bad, she had to go to the hospital. She went in the kitchen and got a glass of water then walked back into the living room like a zombie holding the pills and water in front of her. She calmly sat on the sofa sat the water on the table in front of her opened the pill bottle; then filled her hand. She put five in the hand and laid the rest on the table; she tossed them in her mouth then chased them down with a gulp of water. She picked up five more and chased them down with water. She grabbed a blanket and laid down thinking of Rebecca the only child she loved because she looks so much like her. "I love you Rebe.... A tear slowly rolls its way down her face as her head tilts to the side.

As detectives Pete and Dave enters the scene and crosses the graveyard the other officers had just discovered Jerome's broken body further down the embankment halfway in the water. He looked like a rag doll tossed aside with his limbs twisted in all directions. The impact of the train broke every bone in his body. The coroner was there just in case they found the body before daylight, which they did. He looked the body over determining the impact of the train was the cause of death. They had to put a board under the body to maneuver it in the body bag. His I.D was still on him along with his car keys, which was a good thing because his face was unrecognizable. Everything on him and around him was put in evidence bags. They carefully carried the body up the embankment and handed the bag with his I.D to the detectives; they immediately recognized the name. The train was allowed to go hours ago after they questioned the conductor. The sun was rising after they wrapped everything up. It was a beautiful sunrise as the detectives watched it slowly make its way up. They knew it would be a start of a busy day; but what they didn't know they had a third body waiting to be discovered. They decided to go have breakfast first before they deliver the bad news at the two houses across from each other. Detective Peter looked at his partner Dave as they drove past the houses and said, "How heartbreaking it will be for the husband to find out his wife was murdered by his neighbor. I can't imagine what that is going to be like for him." Dave answered him looking straight ahead, "Like someone ripping your heart out and being filled with rage and pain at the same time. You want to cry and kill the bastard who did it; only to discover somebody else did it for you. The question you should be asking is how do you get through something like that?" Peter looked at Dave and saw his face was hardened with pain, so he asked him, "Is that what happened to you man?" Holding back the tears and memory he softly said, "Yeah, something like that; but I don't want to talk about it so drop it." The rest of the drive to the restaurant was in silence. They ordered breakfast and talked about the two deaths trying to see if there was something, they had in common other than being neighbors. They decided they would go to Greg's house first when they finished eating; they wanted to give Kate some extra sleep time considering she'd been up late worrying about her husband.

Skip, Stanley, James and Doug stood in front of the park answering questions about the man killed by the train. They all had the same answer; they didn't know there was a man on the tracks. They heard the train's whistle blowing long and loud; they thought maybe the train was about to derail so they came to see if the graveyard had been destroyed. When asked why they were at Stanley's house so late; they simply said it was a neighborhood watch meeting going a little late. Daniel was told not to stay because they didn't want him sinning seeing how he found Jesus and all. James saw how well they covered up getting rid of Jerome; he decided right then he has to work hard on getting that contract in St. Petersburg, Fl or he'll be next if he makes one wrong move towards Shannon. Skip held himself together in front of the police; but he quickly left the scene to go to bed he has to pick up Greg in a few hours from the airport. He has to tell his friend his wife is dead because he couldn't get to her in time to save her. He was so distraught about it he didn't notice the detectives talking to Kate in her driveway when he passed by. He just parked his car and went straight in the house showered and went to bed. Before he knew it five o'clock had arrived and he felt like hell. He got up got dressed jumped in the car and headed to the airport; the flashing lights were still at the park but not as many as there were earlier. He cried some of the way thinking what he could have done differently to keep Joyce alive; then there was the affair. How was he going to tell that to his friend? He knew about it but didn't tell Greg about it; now he's got to tell him everything twice he let his friend down. Before he knew it, he was at the airport and Greg was already standing outside waiting for Joyce. Skip stopped the car in front of him jumped out and opened the trunk. Greg was surprised to see Skip, "Morning Skip! What you doing here? Where's my wife? Skip quickly puts Greg's luggage in the trunk and said, "She couldn't make it." His heart started beating fast as he prepares himself to tell all that has happened, "Get in the car man I'll tell you all about it on the way home. They got in the car and Skip started talking fast telling Greg everything that had happened while he was gone; even how they got rid of Romeo. But before he could finish Greg stopped him from talking. He could handle hearing she was killed; but he couldn't take hearing the woman he loved and gave his all and all were having an affair. So many unanswered questions he had about her strange behavior were starting to make sense. Her need for wild sex and her defending Romeo when he told her they will have to kill him. He was so full of rage and pain that he couldn't talk at first; he just cried. Nothing else was said on the rest of the drive home he wouldn't allow Skip to speak. The moment they pulled in the driveway and began unloading the luggage a car pulls up and two detectives get out. "Mr. Hughes? Greg turns and angrily says, "Yes, and you are?" He knew who they were and why they were there. "I'm detective Peter and this is my partner Dave; may we come in to have word with you?" Greg just said, "Yeah, but make it quick I just got in from a long business trip and I am tired." As they walked in Greg looked over at Skip and said, "Thanks bro, I appreciate the ride." Then he yells out, "Honey I'm home; Joyce where you at babe?" Peter interrupted him, "Mr. Hughes please sit down your wife is not here." Greg turns and looks at the detective and asks, "How the hell you know my wife is not here?" Pretending he knows nothing of his wife's demise he asks, "What's this about? Has she done something?" Peter pulls out a photo then hands it to Greg and says, "Your wife is dead Mr. Hughes; we need you to come and identify the body." Greg looks at the picture of his wife's lifeless body lying on the pavement. He nearly loses it, "This is a joke, right?" "Who did this to my baby?" Tears starts flowing as reality set in that the love of his life is gone. He falls down to his knees and began crying uncontrollably unable to stop it. Skip walks over to him and takes the photo out of his hand and gives it to the detective. "I'll bring him there; where is her body?" They give him the address and walks out the door. Skip lifts Greg up saying to him, "Pull it together man you can do this." They meet the detectives at the coroners' office where Greg is taken to the back to identify the body. As her face is revealed he shakes his head to confirm it's her and asks, "Who did this to her?" Peter was too chocked up to say anything, so Dave answered, "Well, your neighbor Jerome Padgett did it; but unfortunately, he's dead too killed by a train last night." Greg looked up at the detective and said, "Lucky train." He kissed Joyce on the forehead and left the room. He got in the car with Skip and said, "The kids come home tonight; man, it's going to be hard telling them their mom is dead." They went home unaware that the detectives were right behind them heading over to tell Kathryn of her husband's demise. Peter still wasn't talking Dave had noticed; so, he said to him, "Man I was right, when you told him his neighbor killed her and was dead also killed by a train. Dude looked at me and said lucky train all I saw was pain and rage in his eyes; but what he doesn't know it's only the beginning." Peter looked at Dave and said, "I don't know how you got through that man; but I'm glad you're okay with it now." They got to Kate's house got out and rang the doorbell but there was no response. They knocked twice and yelled out, "Mrs. Padgett it's detectives Peter and David; but there was no response. The curtains were still pulled opened in the living room, so Peter walked over to look in and to see if she was stirring around. He saw her lying on the sofa partially covered by a blanket and pills spread out on the coffee table. He said to Dave, "I think we have another dead one on our hands, kick in the door!" Dave pulled his gun out and kicks the door open not knowing what to expect he yelled, "Police!" Part of the frame came loose as the door swung open; Steve quickly runs past Dave to the sofa to check to see if Kathryn was still alive, but there was no pulse. Her body was stiff and cold. Dave holster his gun frustrated with finding another dead body he asks, "What the hell is going on around here? That's three bodies from the same neighborhood in less than twenty-four hours; this is no coincident something stinks about this." Greg and Skip ran over as soon as they saw Dave kick in the door. They saw Kate's lifeless body lying on the sofa looking like she was at peace sleeping. Skip yelled out, "Damn, why did she do that?" Dave turned and told them, "Guys I'm sorry you're going to have to leave this area is off limits." They left with no hesitation and went back to Greg's house. Dave called dispatch to send the coroner back to the neighborhood. Peter kneeled down looking in Kate's face asks, "What made her do this not knowing her husband was dead? Something else is going on besides her finding out he killed somebody." Dave walks over and says, "Yeah and we have to dig deep and fast to find the answers." They roped off the area and waited for forensics to come.

Skip left Greg to go give Daniel the news of all that has happened since last night. He called him out of the house to talk because he didn't want Claire and the kids to hear it. By the time Skip finished talking Daniel was in tears hearing about Joyce; he was shocked to find out about Kate taking her own life. After Skip left, he stood outside a while longer trying to figure out how he was going to tell the children both their parents are dead. He knows they wanted to get away from them and be a normal family; but he knows they will always love their parents in spite of their wrong doings that's just how kids are. He was beginning to blame himself for wanting to be a father so bad that he would allow himself to be influenced to take someone else's children. But deep down inside he knew Jerome was going to die sooner or later at the hands of someone else the way his temper was flaring. His death had nothing to do with them taking the children out of harm's way. Skip saw Daniel still standing outside his house trying to process what all has happened. He forgot Daniel is still dealing with the loss of his son; so, he went back to him and convinced him to come over to his house he will help him figure out a better way to tell his family.

Greg went in the bedroom to change clothes finally; he saw a box on the bed with a letter and a key on top. Joyce had written a confession letter to her husband to read to him in person when he got home. It was her way of starting the year off right telling him everything. Greg hesitated to pick up the letter when he saw Joyce handwriting on it; but he decided to pick it up and read it any way.

My dearest darling Greg,

If you are reading this, it's because I was too afraid to talk to you in person.

It is very difficult for me to say this; I have betrayed you by living a double

life. I have been having an affair with Jerome for the past few months. Baby

I am so, so sorry I've done this to you; and I know I am asking too much by

asking you to forgive me. I got lonely as your business trips got longer.

I got involved with Jerome at a time when I was desperate for attention and

I got caught up in a dark place with him. I need you to know that my heart is yours

forever. There was no love between what Jerome, and I shared; I was a lonely

woman looking for attention in all the wrong places. These two weeks you and

I had together alone during the holidays

reminded me why I love you so much.
You let me know there's no one better for me than thee. Please don't let it be
our last time sharing our love with each other; I want more of you for as long
as I can have you. I know you're wondering what's in the box; it's my cash of shame
for being with him. No, I did not sell myself to him I would not take his gifts so
he would give me cash instead. I will do whatever you me to with it; I will even
throw it away if that's what you want me to do consider it done. Please,
Please baby I am begging you not to throw me away for what I've done
to your trust in me. I know your heart is broken but I will do whatever you want to
mend us back together as one. You are my one and only love for the rest
of my LIFE!

LOVE JOYCE

Greg opened the box and saw that it was a lot of cash in high bills in it. He stood up and hurled it across the room and yelled out in rage, "Why couldn't you stay home for just one more night Joyce! All you had to do was stay your ass home one more night!" He shoved all her belongings on the dresser to the floor and began crying again. He decided he needed a drink to calm himself down before the kids get home; he didn't want them to see him this way. But just as he was making his way across the living room heading to the bar the front door swings open. "Daddy we're back!" The children came rushing in like a herd of cattle. Little Triqua asks, "Did ya'll miss us?" But just as they all hugged him, he fell to his knees and cried uncontrollably. They all stood there quiet not sure what to say or do; they've never seen their dad act like this. His parents come in with the luggage and see the children standing around their dad looking at him on his knees crying. His dad asks, "Son you alright? What's going on?" His mom walks over to him gently hugs him and asks, "Is there something we can do to help?" He gets the strength to look up at his kids and say, "Your mom is dead, she was murdered last night." All the children cried out in horror, "Daddy no, it can't be true!" Before he could assure them, it was so Skip walked in. Greg's dad turns to him and asks, "Is it true? Is Joyce really dead?" Skip hesitated at first then answered, "Yes it's true; I had to tell him this morning when I picked him up from the airport." All the children burst out crying surrounding their father hugging him as Skip pulled Greg's parents aside to explain what happened to Joyce. He left a lot of the details out because he didn't want them to know about the affair. He just told them Jerome killed her because he thought she reported him to D.C.F who took their children from them. Which was true but Skip didn't know that; he decided that was the story he would stick with telling.

Barbara stayed all night at the hospital never leaving her baby side, she cried again and realized she had not prayed to God in a long time. She couldn't think of a word to say at first then finally she said, "God if you get my baby through this, I promise I will start back going to church. Please heal my baby I will do anything; please lord, please." James came in with her breakfast just as she finished praying and told her about Joyce as he handed her the food. She ate a little and softly spoke saying, "I can't be worried about anybody right now; I just need my baby to wake up." Shannon walked over to the bed and held Sasha's hand then said, "Please wake up Sasha I got a new book for you to read. Don't leave me please." She turned and ran out of the room to cry. Gwen's mom gave them a ride to the hospital she wanted to see Sasha herself. It brought tears to her eyes to see the frail little body with so many tubes everywhere. She left a vase of flowers said some comforting words to Barbara and left the room crying Shannon left with her. Instead of going in the house Shannon decided to go and talk to Claire. She got there just as Daniel was calling everyone together and telling them the bad news about their parents. They all were sad and cried a little, but Rebecca cried more than any of them. Kate always told Rebecca she loved her she just never said it to the others. Shannon was saddened to hear that Eddy Gal lost both her parents in one night. But she was devastated to hear that Mrs. Joyce was killed by Eddy's dad. Only Shannon and Sasha knew about the affair among the children. Shannon wasn't sure if the kids were happy to be in the custody of Daniel and Claire. She was a bit confused as of to why they were crying when they went through so much trouble to get away from them. Shannon felt that if it were her, she would be happy if both her parents were killed in one night and she would not shed one tear for either of them. She finally got a moment to talk to Claire. "Mrs. Claire, Sasha is in the hospital with rubella. The Doctor says she might not wake up." Shannon starts crying then finish saying, "Please Mrs. Claire can you pray to God not to take her away yet; I need her here with me a little longer I can't do this without her." Claire holds her close and began praying, but all she could say was, "Please Jesus please." Over and over was all she could think to say. There was so much happening at once Claire couldn't think of words to say to comfort anybody.

The next day Shannon found herself going to school without her two best friends and her little Sasha. It's going to be a long day she thought as she slowly made her way to school. She stopped by Sasha's class to let her teacher know Sasha was in the hospital. She really didn't think Mrs. Vinegar would care, but she wanted the class to know why Sasha wasn't there. She slowly started walking to her class with her head down missing her friends. As she approached the bathrooms at the bottom of the stairs, a boy comes out and says to her, "Hi Shannon." She looks up and sees its Darren. "Oh, hey Darren; you're back!" He smiled and said, "Yeah, I am." She asked him, "Is everything okay now?" He looks off as if to find the right words to say, "Yeah, I just have to take it one day at a time." They began walking up the stairs together as he began telling her some of the things he went through while in the mental hospital. He walked her to her class and said he would see her after school smiled and walked away. He felt strange being back around normal people, but his psychologist gave him exercises to do if he felt himself slipping from reality. They weren't sure how long it would take for him to come to terms with Tate's death. They had a hard time getting him to except there wasn't nothing he could have done to keep Tate from doing harm to himself. He is okay with it now, but he still misses his friend.

Daniel and Claire found themselves at a lawyer's office with the children listening to the reading of Kate's will. Everything she had was left to the children there were no mention of Jerome except to say he is to get nothing. She had already planned and paid for her funeral arrangements after Jerome beat her up and put her in the hospital the last time. But there was one action Kate took that shocked everybody in the room. She had her lawyer draw papers giving Daniel and Claire full legal custody of the children. She said she watched Claire daily suffer from losing one child. If anyone deserves a second chance at being a mother, it's Claire. No one in Jerome's family or hers is to get her kids should anything happen to her. The house in Jamaica is left to Rebecca because she reminds me of the sweet little girl I once was, I was not always a bad person. The lawyer set a date for Daniel and Claire to come back so he could go over the legal papers with them. They left the lawyers office and went straight to the funeral home. It was there they discovered there was no insurance or money to bury Jerome. Daniel told the director they will bury Kate first then would deal with Jerome after that. The director agreed and they set Kate's service for the next day she left nothing for the children to decide concerning her funeral, all they needed to do was show up. Just as they were leaving Greg and his kids were coming in to take care of Joyce final arrangements. He had the cash box with him; the children thought it was something special he wanted their mom to have before she is laid to rest. They still can't believe their mom is gone; this is not a good start of a new year for them. Joyce sister came along to help Greg and the children get through the process of making the arrangements. She wanted to dress her sister, but Greg wouldn't allow it; he insisted on dressing his wife himself. He was no longer in rage about his wife's death; he knew he had to pull himself together and be strong for the children's sake. He sat them all down and had a heart to heart talk with them on how hard it was going to be for them all to deal with the loss of their mom. He told them he would be moving them to the central Florida area to be around the love and support of his family. He told them he needs his family help too. They all agreed to leave as soon as the school year ends in May. The children waited in the lobby as Greg and their Aunt went in the back. It was quiet at first with a few sniffles every now and then. Michael started talking about some of the good pool parties Joyce would plan for them and how much she went out of her way to make them happy. One by one they began sharing the fun memories about their mom until their laughter filled the lobby. It was the first time they were able to talk about their mom without crying. Greg was glad to see them smiling again as he was coming from the back, he smiled at them then went into the office and closed the door for privacy. He presented the box to the funeral director and told him to use the cash to bury Jerome. He told the director it was collected to be given to him while he was alive; but since he was killed before it was given to him, please use it to bury him instead. After Greg and his family left the director counted the cash and said out loud, "Yep, just enough to give Mr. Padgett a decent burial." He gets up calls out to his assistant, "Prep Mr. Padgett's body he's going to get buried after all." He called Daniel and Claire to let them know Jerome's funeral was paid for by a generous donation; he assured them both bodies will be ready for tomorrow's service. The next day the service was held at Claire's small church on the corner in the neighborhood. Since most of the people lived nearby, they all walked to the church. The small church was packed; there was barely enough room for both coffins to fit in the front. The service was short because Kate arranged for her body to be laid to rest by her parents in Texas. Jerome's body was laid to rest at the local cemetery in a plot his family members chose. Even though Kate's intention was to leave Jerome with nothing; in the end it was her money that paid for his funeral.

Saturday morning at 11a.m is the time of service Joyce home going will began. Her service will be held at the large Baptist church near downtown because everybody is attending it. Even the prostitutes who tried to save her came along with the owner of the club. There was not a single person at home or on the streets in both neighborhoods. Much was said about how she loved all the children hanging out at her house; and she had the best parties. She was loved by many so much so till there was not a dry eye in the service; it was a long three-hour service, but nobody complained. Greg and the children were glad it was over all they wanted to do was get home and cry. Greg held it together until everyone was gone and the children were finally in bed. He went in his room and sat on the bed and began reading the letter that his wife wrote her last words to him

CHAPTER FIVE

After Shannon told Mrs. Vinegar about Sasha's illness, she went to talk to principle Bailey about taking the class to the hospital to see Sasha as a field trip. He gave the okay and began making arrangements for transportation. After lunch Mrs. Vinegar had the class make cards as each child got up to go out the door heading home, she handed them a note asking each parent to buy a balloon to send to the hospital for a sick child. The next morning, they were on the bus heading to the hospital to see their classmate. Sasha was out of I.C.U and in a regular room but was still in a comma. As the children came in the hospital with their animal shaped balloons, the doctor told them to talk to Sasha as if she could hear them. They are hoping familiar voices will help bring her out of the comma. The balloons and cards filled the room along with the fresh flowers she was getting every day. They all told Sasha they miss her, and they want her to get better to come back to school; but they all left the room crying. By the time they got on the bus they had many questions to ask Mrs. Vinegar to answer like: What is rubella? Why is she still sleeping? Is she dying? When will she be coming back to school? They were back to acting like first graders. Two days later Sasha woke up crying, she didn't know where she was. Barbara was sleep in the bed next to her; she got up to calm Sasha down, "it's okay baby mommy's here." Barb started crying, she was so happy Sasha finally woke up. Sasha tried getting up but couldn't because of all the tubes connected to her. She started pulling at some of them to get them off but that only made the machines alarms sound off. Doctors and nurses came running from every direction into her room. Sasha really started panicking because she didn't know who they were. Barb explained to her that she is in the hospital because she is very sick. She calmed down enough to allow them to remove some the tubes; but she was still weak from being in a comma for over a week. The doctor ordered the nurse to draw blood to take to the lab to make sure the rubella was clear of her system. Three hours later the results came back clear, and the doctor explained to barb the side effects Sasha were going to experience. "Her eyesight has been affected so she will need glasses. You will have to get her ears checked twice a year because of the excess wax build up she will be experiencing; she will need a specialist to flush her ears. We will be keeping her here for a few more days to make sure she gets her strength back." Barb was happy the nightmare was over; she couldn't bear losing another child. Sasha was back in her room enjoying all the different animal balloons her classmates got her. She asked Barb, "Where did all these balloons come from mommy?" Barb smiled and said, "All the children in your class bought them here for you two days ago. The school arranged for it to be a field trip for them because they all wanted to see you; they really miss you." Sasha looked at all the colorful cards with her name on them and said, "I don't remember them being here; but I'm glad they came." She played with as many balloons as she could and tried to read every card; but she was too tired and ended up falling asleep with a card and a balloon in her hand. Barb saw that she was asleep and decided to go and get something to eat and rest herself. Four days later Sasha was released from the hospital and came home to a quiet house. Shannon and little James were in school; she could move around but not too much she would still get a little weak. She took a long nap but woke up in time to see Shannon come home from school. She was so happy to see her big sister; they hugged each other tight and the first thing Sasha asked, "Where's the new book you bought me? I can't wait for us to read it!" Shannon surprisingly asked, "You heard me? Wow!" Sasha answered, "I heard a few people, but nobody heard me; but then I realized I couldn't talk so I stopped listening." They both giggled for a little while. Shannon hugged Sasha again and said, "I have some bad news to tell you. She told Sasha all about Joyce and Eddy's parents being killed the night she got sick. The one good news she mentioned was that Darren came back to school. "Wow! I missed a lot in two weeks; I'm never getting sick again." Shannon laughed picked up the book and sat on the bed then began reading to Sasha; she really missed having her around. As the weeks passed all the children was beginning to settle in their new normal activities. To overcome their grief, they began hanging out over to Claire's house. Claire was teaching them about the love of God and how he can mend their broken hearts. They enjoyed Claire teaching them about God's love; so, they started going to church with her on Sunday and Tuesday night bible study. Sasha was really into learning about the love of God; she began telling everybody she was going to be just like Jesus when she grows up. The way she sees it; Jesus makes people happy when they are sad and that is what she is going to do. Easter is coming up and Claire was preparing the children to do a play and quote poems for the occasion. All the parents joined in to help with rehearsals, props and whatever was needed to make it a success for the children. The event would be taking place at the bigger church in Delray Beach; it was bigger plus it had a lot of land for the Easter egg hunt after service. The teens and pre-teens were doing the resurrection play. The role of Jesus was given to Darren he gladly accepted the role; it made him feel important. Barbara became a member at the small church she felt she needed some help from God. Her husband James was still looking to get a job in St Petersburg; but Barb knew why he was trying to move them away; she overheard him threaten Shannon again. That's what made her join the church, she even started acting normal and reading the bible at home. She started teaching her girls how to pray for people and for themselves. The girls were alright with seeing their mom acting okay for now. They know she has moments of being normal for a while then something comes along and knocks her back in the "crazy zone"; that's what Shannon calls it. Everyone was so excited about the Easter play; before they knew it, they were doing final rehearsal. Claire was giving the announcements of the activities that would take place after service. The main event was the big Easter egg hunt that has lots of cash and prizes. Everybody yelled out cheerfully at the news of that except Sasha; she stood up and said, "Excuse me Mrs. Claire I can't do Easter egg hunt. They all quieted down to hear her reason thinking maybe something serious happened to her during an Easter egg hunt. Claire, sounding as sympathetic as she could ask, "Sasha why can't you do the Easter egg hunt sweetie?" They all looked at Barb for the answer, but she was clueless too; so, they wait to hear the devastating story as to why she can't go hunt eggs. Sasha with a serious look on her face burst out and says, "Because Jesus wasn't raised a bunny rabbit and rabbits don't lay eggs! There's something wrong with that rabbit I tell ya! The church was filled with laughter and a sigh of relief that it wasn't something serious; Wanda and Eddy looked at Shannon and said, "That's your little sister," and laughed even harder. Stan was there watching the rehearsals; he'd gotten attached to the families in his neighborhood. He was a rich man living alone in his big house on the hill. He didn't care to socialize much with his own family until being around the families here. He plans to spend the summer getting to know his family again. He realizes life is short and family is everything. He took everyone out to dinner after rehearsal and paid the bill. He promised the children he would come see them perform on Easter Sunday.

Easter morning was upon them before they knew it. Many of the parents went to sunrise service in the park at the end of the street. They all bought fresh flowers to place on Tate's grave when service was over. The children were up and excited about the event of the day; it was all about them. Stan had a couple of charter buses lined up in the neighborhood to get as many people there who didn't have transportation or who didn't want to drive. Both buses were loaded as they head to Delray to celebrate Easter; Stan did not get on the bus as his limo leads the way there. The children were dressed sharp and pretty in bright colors with their baskets; Sasha of course wasn't having it with a basket, Easter is about Jesus not a bunny basket. Barbara stopped trying to explain it to her and let her go on with her Jesus: after all it's not every day a six-year-old gets stuck on Jesus. Shannon told everybody to please not ask her where her basket is. They got to church on time and performed; the program was a success. Stan hired a photographer to take pictures of each family together; he left right after the program was over, good thing he did. The preacher of the hosting church decided he would call a prayer line before the egg hunt began. The children would be first of course to make sure they are protected. Something strange happened to Barbara's kids as they went through the prayer line; it's like God opened their eyes to see the true nature of some of the members in the church, or maybe God was just being funny. Shannon sat down and looked up at the pastor as he was praying for people and saw he had a rabbit's head. She rubbed her eyes and kept them closed for a few seconds thinking maybe some of the crazy stuff Sasha be saying is starting to get in her head. She opened her eyes only to see a big rabbit head on a man's body. She turned her head to look away and saw four female rabbits with quite a few little rabbits on a couple benches to her left. She grabbed Sasha by the hand and said, "The pastor got a head of a rabbit and there are little ones up front on the left." Sasha being small stood up on the seat to take a look and lets out a high-pitched scream. Shannon quickly pulls her down and asks, "Did you see them?" Sasha looking like she saw a ghost said, "NO, but I saw the men sitting near them looking like wolves growling with their teeth showing." Just as she said that James Jr. let's out a yelp and said, "Snakes, these people has snake heads on their feet!" The people sitting in front of them turned around to shhh them quiet. Shannon couldn't believe what she was hearing; so, she turned to ask her mom what was going on only to find her gone. She looks up and saw their mom at the front of the prayer line. She jumps up out of her seat grabs Sasha and James by the hand and takes off running to the front of the line yelling, "Don't let that rabbit put his hands on my mama!" Barbara raised her arms in the air praising the lord waiting for the pastor to lay his hand on her forehead. Shannon makes it to Barbara just as the pastor is about to lay his hand on her head. Shannon kicks the pastor on the shin as hard as she could. The pastor lets out a yell and bends down to grab his leg and looks at Shannon and yells, "What's wrong with you!" Barbara passes out just as Shannon kicks the pastor on the other shin and they both hit the floor at the same time. The deacons run over to see what was going on with their pastor. Sasha screams out, "Wolves, wolves are attacking" an ear-piercing scream follows just as James starts jumping on the men feet yelling, "Snakes!" The women ushers try to get to Barb to put a cloth over her while she is on the floor; but little James is stomping on their feet yelling snakes if they come near Barb. The pastor is finally able to get up and he tries to calm them down; but just as he steps towards them Shannon lays the hardest kick, she could give on his shin again sending him down to the floor moaning in agony. The deacons tried to grab them, but Shannon kept kicking, James was still stomping, and Sasha's screams was becoming unbearable. Claire was able to finally make her way up there to find out what was going on with the children. She managed to calm them down just as Barbara began to wake up and they both ask at the same time, "What is going on?" Shannon turned around and looked at the both of them as Claire helped Barbara get up and said, "That preacher has a rabbit head." Little James grabs his mom's hand pointed at the ushers and the deacons and said, "Their feet are snakes." Sasha pointing at the deacons screams out, "They are wolves and I wanna go home!" Daniel came to help Claire get Barbara and her children out of the Church. Skip and their father James went up to apologize for the children causing such a ruckus during prayer service. The pastor was so furious he just yelled at them as they walked quickly towards the door, "Get them out of my church and don't come back!" Everybody else stood up and ran towards the door laughing hysterically. They all made it to the bus to find Sasha crying, Shannon so embarrassed she was trying to cover her face; and little James not even caring what happened, he was jumping in the seat. The bus driver got on the bus last announced between his laughing fits, "That was the best prayer line I've ever been in; I'm going to remember this Easter." He was laughing so hard he had tears coming from his eyes. Wanda and Eddy Gal rushed to the back of the bus to try and comfort their friend through her most embarrassing moment without laughing. Big James, Daniel and Claire didn't know what to say to Barbara at first until she broke the silence by asking, "Why is everybody laughing so much? Why was that pastor so angry at us?" They told Barbara what happened after she passed out. She couldn't believe what she was hearing; then she looked back at her kids and said, "OH lawdy, lawdy." Daniel just said, "Out of the mouths of babes." Claire chuckled a little and said, "Well one thing for sure though; they didn't let that big head rabbit touch their mom." Everybody on the bus quieted down to hear the children tell what happened from their point of view. By the time the bus reached the neighborhood they all had sore cheeks and stomach form laughing so hard. Shannon was still feeling a bit embarrassed about the whole thing; but Sasha was just glad it was over because she didn't like the idea of that rabbit being on Jesus Easter any way.

Monday morning at school started with the children talking about how good the Easter play was; especially the great performance Darren did playing Jesus. The highlight of the conversation was the prayer line as the children on the other bus was hearing of it for the first time. The hallway was full of laughter until they saw Miss. Belinda come walking out of the office. They all got quiet not sure what to say to her as she approached them. Sasha didn't know why all of a sudden everybody stopped talking; so she squeezed her way through the crowd to see what was happening. When she saw it was Miss. Belinda coming towards them; she got so excited and yelled out to her as she got close, "Hey Miss. Pussy lips! It is so good to see you back to school!" Shannon, Wanda and Eddy's mouth just dropped open with disbelief at what they just heard. Belinda turned to look at them not sure of what she just heard and ask, "What was that?" Before Sasha could repeat it somebody in the crowd yelled out, "Hey Miss. Belinda, welcome back to school." Shannon put her hand over Sasha's mouth while the others gathered around Belinda to shake her hand and welcome her back. Belinda smiled and shed a few tears because she was touched by the children being so kind in welcoming her back. As she disappeared up the stairs they all turned to Sasha to say, "That is not her name; why did you call her that? Sasha simply replied, "Because that's the name ya'll call her when ya'll talk about her." Wanda kneeled down to her doing what her mom use to do, said to her, "Oh sweet Sasha, they called her that name being mean; my mom told us never call her that again. It's not good to call people bad names; her real name is Miss. Belinda." Sasha smiled and said, "Ooh, I like that name; it sounds prettier than pussy lips. I really didn't like that name any way thank you Wanda." She turned to the others and yelled, "You guys were really mean to her, shame on you!" They all laughed as the bell rang for class to start. As they walked to their class Shannon said to Wanda, "Girl, you reminded me of your mom back there the way you talked to Sasha." Wanda smiled and said, "Yeah, she would've handled it just like that too; I miss her so much."

It was a good start of the school week for Sasha, no problem with teacher or classmates. She was finally feeling like she belonged there. That feeling came crashing down as she got home from school to hear her dad tell her mom he got the job in St. Petersburg building houses. They will be moving the second week of May just before school gets out. Sasha ran to her room not believing what she just heard. She sat on the bed and cried a little. "Oh no, this is not going to be good for us," she whispered softly to herself. She knew once they leave Boynton it will no longer be safe for Shannon. Barbara argued with James about the move; she just did not want to move. After he pointed out the fact that she really didn't have a reason to stay since her best friend was killed. The thought of losing Joyce was hurtful enough; but the thought of not having a man in her life was not an option so she agreed to move. She knows once they leave there she's really going to have to work hard at keeping him away from Shannon. The picture of her daughter's battered body still was fresh floating in her head. She still had not come to terms with that; then the crazy voices started whispering in her head as she started feeling her sanity slip away. There were no crazy episodes with Joyce; she kept her busy and made sure she was being good to the kids. Joyce is gone now and the thought of moving to a new place is causing her to unravel; but that's what James is counting on. He is hoping she will lose it enough for him to put her in a hospital then Shannon will be his.

As soon as Shannon walk in the back door into the room Sasha told her what she overheard. "I don't want to move Shannon I like it here." Shannon throws her books on the bed as the smile she had fades away. She started to panic but then decided to go check with her mom to make sure it was true. She comes into the living room to see her mom sitting on the sofa with her head down. Before she could ask about the move her mom starts talking, "Your dad has a job in St Petersburg; we'll be moving there in a few weeks." Fear and sadness came over Shannon as the word moving entered her mind. This place has become her safe haven. If they move the people in the other places will not care about what happens to her. Her voice tremors as she is finally able to ask, "Can we just not move with him for a change? Why do we have to go with him all the time?" Barbara got so angry at the fact that Shannon would ask her not to be with her husband; enraged she answers, "Because he makes the money to take care of us, that's why!" Shannon ran back to the room crying before Barb could say anything else. Sasha knew it was true when Shannon came in crying; so she started back crying and asks, "What are we going to do now?" Shannon still sobbing says, "There's nothing we can do; we're children and have to do what we are told." Little James walks in to see his sister's crying and ask, "What ya'll cryin bout now?" Sasha answer, "We're moving to St Pete –a-bug." Shannon laughs with tears rolling down her face and corrects her, "It's Saint-Peters-burg; I need to work on you pronunciations little girl." Little James sadly says, "Awe naw, he we go agin." Shannon just shook her head at how he just miss-pronounced that whole sentence then said, "There's just no hope for you boy." They went to the living room to talk to their mom with hopes of seeing if there was any way they didn't have to move; but she was gone, and so was their dad. Shannon walks over to the front door and locked it saying, "Come on guys lets go over to Wanda's house until they decide to come home." They got to Wanda's house to see Mr. Greg packing big boxes with the front door open. "Come on in they're in the den having pizza; go have some if there's any left." They ran to the den and grabbed some pizza; there were still some slices left for them. Shannon sat next to Wanda to tell her the bad news. Wanda looks at her starts crying and said, "We're moving next week because daddy is not handling himself well without mom. So he's moving us to Sanford with grandpa and grandma to help him through it. I'm going to miss you Shannon; you're my bestest friend I ever had; I hope I never forget you." Shannon eyes fill up with tears as she says, "I know I won't forget you or your parents for treating us like family. I don't think I will be protected there like I am here; I'm scared. I know my dad still doesn't like me; he wants to hurt me again. Mom is going into her crazy zone she won't be able to stop him; I wish I was born into another family." Wanda realized her crying about moving was nothing compared to what her friend was facing. "Well you have Jesus on your side now Shannon; just believe he won't let anything bad happen to you again." With tears rolling down her face Shannon said, "I will believe with all my heart and pray Jesus will stop him." They finished eating and began packing boxes. Shannon noticed there were not any of Mrs. Joyce pretty things in the house so she ask, "Wanda what happened to your mom things?" Wanda answers, "Oh dad had the salvation army come by and pick up most of it. Her good jewelry he gave to me and my sisters; but he kept a few things that were special to him even the letter she wrote. He keeps reading it over and over; I hope grandma and grandpa can help. I'm not use to seeing my dad act so strange. With thirteen kids helping with the packing all the boxes were full in no time and the house was looking empty. They all sadly looked around at the bare walls that once had pictures and paintings on them. Shannon and Wanda had just taken a box in the garage when Stan, Skip and Daniel walked up to them. The girls spoke and told the guys how much they will miss being around them. Stanley asked Shannon, "Are you moving too? Sadly Shannon answers, "Yes sir, I wish I wasn't though. Mr. Stanley you don't act like most rich people if you don't mind me saying. Why do you like being around us?" He smiled and said, "Because all of you are like family to me." He knew why she didn't want to move; she was special to everybody. If it wasn't for her the neighborhood wouldn't have come together like it did. "Don't be so sad about moving Shannon good people are everywhere not just here. I'm sure someone will be there to keep you safe just like we have here." She smiled a little and shook his hand to say, "Thank you Mr. Stanley, I hope the people are as nice." She was about to walk away but Stanley stopped her and asked, "Where are you guys moving to?" "Mom said St. Petersburg; my dad will be building houses there." With a big smile on his face Stan says, "That's a beautiful place to live; if I travel that way I may drop by and pay you a visit. Would that be okay?" She answers him, "Sure thing Mr. Stanley that would be great." She walks away with a big smile on her face. The moment the girls walk into the house Stanley says to the guys, "That man is going to kill that little girl the first chance he gets; but I'm going to make sure that doesn't happen." It was the first time they saw Stanley get angry; but before they could say anything he switched the conversation to talking about Greg. They went in to check on their friend to have a few more laughs and drinks for the last time.

The week went by too fast as far as Shannon was concerned; she wanted it to slow down so she could spend as much time with Wanda and Eddy Gal as she could. By Saturday morning the moving truck was at Greg's house loading all the boxes and furniture. He was going to stay at the hotel for his last two days but Stan told him to stay with him until they leave. There were not much to pack at Shannon's house mostly clothes and a small amount of new furniture he bought while Barbara was in the hospital. James always got furnished places to stay in until the next move; this place was not furnished so they move in with old stuff. He made sure his brother knew where he was moving to in case he wants to visit. He intentionally did not tell the other guys he was moving; he wanted to get as far away from them. Once he knew he had the job he stopped going to the meetings; he figure he would just leave without them knowing nothing, forgetting all about the fact that kids tell everything to everybody. Stan already knew the company he would be working for and already sent Doug to St. Pete. If James had been at the last few meetings he would've noticed Doug was missing. Sunday night was especially sad for Eddy Gal; she was spending the last few hours with her two best friends in the whole world. They shared their best memories, cried and made promises to write. They held each other in a group hug for the last time then tearfully parted ways. Monday morning the movers came to load the small amount of furniture while Robert came to take his brother to catch the bus to St. Pete. The girls weren't happy about moving; and little James didn't care one way or the other because he was going to have the same problem in school no matter where they moved to. Barbara wasn't doing well at all mentally; she started doing weird motions with her fingers and mumbling conversations with the voices in her head. When Shannon saw they were catching the bus and noticed her mom acting strange; she knew it was going to be a long dreadful trip. It was fun at first stopping in different city stations to grab a bite to eat and use the bathroom; but it all went sour the moment they had to change over to another bus at a station that was in a rough looking neighborhood. The other bus was late and the station closed early as it was getting dark; it was four hours of terror according to Shannon and Sasha. They kept hearing all kinds of creepy noises coming from the small patch of trees next to the station. Their dad James had them hiding in the dark shadows every time a car would pass by every now and then; he regrets traveling the cheap way now; it's putting his family at risk. Finally he saw the headlights of the bus coming towards them; he told them to stand under the street light so the driver would see them while he gets their luggage. He has all the bags in place by the time the driver stops the bus and gave him their tickets as soon as the driver stepped out to open the side to load the luggage. The girls wasted no time getting on and finding a seat right away considering not too many people took the bus in the evening during the week. They made it to St. Petersburg after midnight and took a taxi to the hotel that was being paid by James new job until he finds a place to stay. They had two rooms with an adjoining door between them; no one unpacked they just crawled in their beds and went to sleep. James got up early ate breakfast at the buffet then headed to work before Barb and the kids got up. Barb got her and the kids down to eat before breakfast was over; she ate a little then went to front desk to get information on how to get to key places she needed to go to. She couldn't drive and didn't like taking a cab because she didn't know how to tell them where she needed to go; so she would walk and it didn't matter how far it was. The clerk asks if she needs her to call a cab; Barb just said no and went back to the table with the kids. Little James just sat down with his third plate of food with the girls watching and telling him he was going to get sick from eating too much. Barbara pointed to a window telling them the direction they needed to go to get to the stores and a mall. Shannon said to little James, "Eat up you're going to need it for energy if it's a long walk." He shoveled the food down so fast till he almost chocked as always; Barb slapped him on the back then told him to slow down as she got up and headed for the door. Shannon grabbed Sasha by the hand so she wouldn't get left behind as she ran after their mom to catch up. Barbara walked so fast her kids were always running to keep up or she left them; she only cared about getting where she needed to go as fast as she could get there. Lucky for them she walked to the mall which was only two miles from the hotel. They were glad to be out of the heat and not running as their mom slowed down to do some window shopping at a few stores. She was about halfway in the mall when she heard someone call her by her maiden name, "Barbara Bryant is that you?" Barb turned to see who in St. Pete would know her by her maiden name. She recognized the face immediately; it was an old friend from home. "Susie, oh my God it's good to see you; how long have you been here?" They hugged each other smiling as Susie answered, "I've been here twenty years so far; and how are you doing Barb? Are these little ones yours? They are so cute." Barb answered, "I'm doing okay; we just moved here last night my husband just started a new job here. I'm out trying to find my way around before I start looking for a place to stay; we're at the hotel for now and yes these are my little brats." They began walking together slowly through the mall exchanging information before finally finding a place to sit down. They talked for two hours catching up on times past then Sue offered to take them back to the hotel; as they said good bye Sue said she would come back the next day to take Barb around to look for a place to stay. Shannon was happy because it meant they would be staying at the hotel and not running in the hot sun from place to place. The next morning Sue came by to sit and have breakfast with Barb and the kids before going out to look for places to live. Barb told her where James job site was to give her general idea where to look that was close to his job since they didn't have a vehicle. They had only been looking for two weeks when they got lucky and found a place; or maybe it was a blessing. It was in Sue's neighborhood; it was by luck, grace or a blessing. Susie mentioned to her Pastor that she was helping a friend look for a place to stay; wouldn't you know her Pastor just happens to have an apartment for rent. He owned five acres and built two apartment builds on the back part of the property not far from his house. There were only two apartments per building because he didn't want too many tenants taking up his time from the lord; a two story apartment building one upstairs and one down stairs on each. His church was the biggest building in the neighborhood where everybody called him preacher Butler. He was father to two cute little girls ages eight and four; his wife is the sweetest first lady you would ever know as the congregation put it. He told Sue to bring her friend by so he could meet her to see if she would be a good tenant to rent to. He talked with Barb for a moment then took her to view the upstairs apartment because it was the only one left empty; he'd just rented out the bottom one two days before to three nice young good looking professional men. It was a three bedroom two bath very spacious apartment. It was larger than the duplex they had in Boynton and it was walking distance from James job. An alley was the entrance to the apartments that separated the Butler's property from the houses across the street. It was also the only access the tenants had to get to their place without having to use the driveway at the main house. Preacher Butler put a fence and a garden of angel statues which he called his garden of angels in the back to separate the house from the apartments; he put a gate on the fence to give him access so he wouldn't have to walk around the block. He took Barb back to the house where he had her fill out the lease and told her to come back and pick up the keys next week. Barb was excited about telling James about the place she found for them when he came in from work. Sue came back that evening to take them both over to see the place together. James loved it because he could walk to work and it was close to good fishing as he was told when Sue found out he loves fishing. The furniture was delivered two days after James notified the moving company that had it in storage; it's the part of moving Barbara doesn't like unpacking. Lucky for her the children are big enough now to help unpack their own things except Sasha. Every since Sasha was sick and almost died Barb wouldn't allow her to do much of anything around the house; she was afraid she would get in harm's way and she couldn't bear to lose another child. The three guys in the apartment below them was Doug and two of his partners who helped him set up surveillance equipment inside James apartment to make sure no harm will come to Shannon without him knowing. Was it luck that Barb chose to move in the same apartment building Doug found to stay in while he's there in St. Pete? Doug sure felt like it was luck for him; he knew he could not be seen by his new neighbors but made sure the other two guys would be seen by everybody to keep nosey neighbors away. As soon as the unpacking was done Sue took Barb to register the children in school so she wouldn't have to bother with it when it started. Barb being herself put the kids in summer school to get them out of the house and away from her. Shannon didn't like that though; she made plans to explore the new city they moved in to get to know the kids so she wouldn't be labeled new kid when school starts. She did notice that so far they had not come across any gangs yet; she really was not in the mood for fighting. She was more than glad not to be seeing much of their dad; he was leaving to go to work before they wake up and was coming home when they were gone to bed. Sasha got to know the two Butler girls as they would always meet in the garden to play. The girls love playing around the statues but Sasha didn't like them at all. She said some of them had bad spirits in them saying bad things about people. She would always run through the garden as fast as she could so she wouldn't hear them talking. Sasha's spiritual encounters began when she was sick with rubella. She told Shannon the reason she didn't wake up right away was because she didn't want to come back to her life here. She was in a beautiful peaceful place with flowers so big it made her look as small as an ant. They had pretty colors she'd never seen before here; and they smelled so good you could taste the sweetness in your mouth every time you inhaled the fragrance. Sasha said she had so much fun playing with the angels all day until one very tall one came to take her home; but the angel had a hard time getting her to go home because she said she had bad parents. She only agreed to go after she had the angels to promise they would come to visit her. Shannon didn't believe her at first until she woke up one night and saw Sasha talking to a bright figure sitting on the bed; but it quickly disappeared when she moved to get a closer look. When Shannon asked what was it Sasha simply said it was her angel friend who tells her good stories about God. Shannon figured God must have given Sasha a special gift for being sick; so when Sasha told her about the talking statues she believed her. Preacher Butler love having Sasha over playing with his girls keeping them busy while he studied the word of God. He knew Sasha was not an average kid by the questions she would ask him about the bible; he told her she was too smart for her own good. Now when she told him about the bad talking angel statues in his garden he just brushed it off as a child's imagination. One day while he sat on a bench between two statues meditating he felt the hairs rise on the back of his neck; and heard some strange growling sound in the breeze blowing around him. At that moment Sasha is on her way over to visit the girls doing her usual run through the garden to get past the statues. Just as she is approaching the area where preacher Butler is sitting; she lets out a loud screeching, "Aaaaahhh, preacher Butler look out!" He hears a deep evil voice say to him, "Go away!" He jumps away just as Sasha screams to him to look out; a statue falls on the bench where he was sitting. He runs over to Sasha picks her up and runs towards the house. As he gets to the door he looks back and ask her, "Was that one of the bad ones saying bad things?" She answered, "Yes sir, I told you they were bad; they do not like you." He put her down and said, "Yes you did; now can you point out the ones that have a bad spirit? She showed him all the ones that were bad then ran off to play. Chills came over him as he realized most of his beautiful angels were evil. All this time he thought kids were sneaking his in yard turning them the wrong way. Two days later as Sasha and his girls came home from school they saw there were a lot of angels missing from the garden; he only kept the four Sasha said were good. Fresh sod and flowers filled in the barren spots along with a few concrete benches. Preacher Butler asked Barbara if he could start taking Shannon and Sasha to church with him and his family. Of course Barbara agreed in fact she told him to take all three; but little James wanted nothing to do with going to a strange church since Easter. Barbara started acting like her old self again; not caring for her children. James was noticing she wasn't watching over Shannon as much anymore; but he was still too busy working over time. He knows eventually the work will slow down and he will be able to make Shannon pay for getting him beat in Boynton. James never got the chance to meet his land lord or his neighbors below; he's been working too hard to think about meeting them. When the work slows down he plans to meet them and to see if any of them like fishing; he could use a good fishing buddy.

Summer school ended so the kids got in the last part of vacation bible school at church to get away from Barb and her crazy moments. They love doing craft projects and art work that pertained to learning the bible stories. Preacher Butler got them involved in some of the community programs to get to know the other kids in the neighborhood. He discovered Shannon was the brain behind Sasha; she love motivating kids to do better. Preacher Butler admired the way Shannon got more people involved in helping the church reach more people in the community. The last event of the vacation bible school was a festival that included a gospel concert on Saturday night. Everybody participated in putting posters everywhere; announcements of the event were being called in to local radio stations to get the word out. Tickets were sold out for Friday's festival and Saturday night's concert; the church was packed. Barbara sent the kids to church with pastor and his family as she decided not to go to the concert. They left early so Preacher Butler could open the church and get everything set for the concert. A few groups started arriving early to set up their instruments on stage; one of whom was the pastor's best friends the Divine Brothers. They are conjoined twins joined at the head whose been singing since they were teenagers. As pastor was walking down the aisle with the girls toward the stage the twins came down to greet their friend that they had not seen in a while. As they got closer Sasha looked up at the two tall thin men coming and said, "Oh, wow!" Pastor looked down at her and said, "Yeah, they do look alike don't they?" Sasha looking puzzled didn't know why pastor said they looked alike; that's not what she was seeing. Finally she said, "I was talking about the beautiful angel walking with them." Pastor asks, "Is it a good one or a bad one? "I don't know," she said surprisingly. "I've never seen that one before, I'll ask him." Before he could ask another question the twins were greeting him handshakes and hugs taking turns speaking to say, "Butler, God has blessed us to see each other one more time; it's good to see you brother." Pastor introduced them to Sasha and Shannon as they said hello to the girls at the same time; that made Sasha giggle. Shannon and the Butler girls went up front to sit down while pastor and Sasha talked with the twins. Sasha had a lot of questions she asked the twins that they kindly answered; she then said to them, "You have a beautiful angel with you; did you know that?" "One of them answered, "No, but I'm glad God has allowed you to see him and let us know that we are blessed to have one." They kneeled down and gave her hug and said to her, "You are a special little one that God has given a special gift to see angels." "Thank you," she said to them, but she wasn't smiling any more. The men talked a little more prayed with pastor Butler then went back on stage. Pastor took Sasha by the hand and started walking to the front where the others were. He said to Sasha, "Was that fun meeting two people that looked alike?" Sasha sadly answered, "No sir not at all." He stopped and kneeled down to see Sasha was crying and asks, "What's wrong Sasha? Did you see something else?" She hesitated a little and answered, "The angel told me God sent him to bring them home to him tonight in heaven. He said they were very good men; but I don't understand that." Pastor Butler was at a loss of words he didn't know what to say to her or what to think himself of possibly losing his friends; so he brushed it off and said, "Come on let's get you to your sister I have to open service." As he was walking away from the children he prayed, "God please don't let that be true, please." Two local groups opened the concert to get the people excited for more to come. The twins was third to sing because they had to leave early so they could make it to the next state to rest before singing on Sunday morning. Each group was giving time to sing three songs; by the third song the twins started singing it was looking like a tent revival. People started coming up to the stage getting happy and calling on Jesus. The Divine Brothers was sounding like a heavenly choir on stage and God had made an alter call. Butler had planned to catch the twins behind stage to tell them what Sasha had told him; but he was so busy praying for people that by the time it was over the twins had already left the concert. Pastor Butler was disappointed he couldn't get to his friends as the evening passed and he was starting to feel sad about it; he couldn't say it was just a little girl's imagination. They got home before it was late as he dropped Barbs kids at their house and drove through the back gate through the garden to his house. The first thing he did was call the hotel to catch his friends before they leave; he was happy and surprised they answered. They told him they couldn't talk long because they were on their way out; so he prayed a prayer of protection with them instead and hung up the phone. He couldn't bring himself to tell them what the little girl said, so he let out a sigh of relief and took a shower. Twenty five minutes later he turns on the TV to see breaking news of a bad accident that has the highway shut down near the air port. His heart sinks as he has a feeling he knows the people that are in it. When the reporter says two people has been flown to the hospital; Butler waste no time getting dressed and head out to the hospital. As he is driving he is crying and praying once again for God to save his friends; but as he pulls in the parking lot it comes to him what Sasha said, "They were very good men so God was bringing them home." He parked the car dried his tears , grabbed his bible and white collar and went inside the emergency rooms to look for them. He asked a nurse that was passing by where were the two accident victims that was flown in by helicopter; she pointed to the room then rushed into another. He quickly walks to the room and gets there just as the doctors are coming out; he asks, "Are they going to survive?" They look at him and see the white collar and sadly say, "No pastor, their head injuries were unlike anything we've ever seen in an accident before; it was too severe. Do you know the family? Butler was a little choked for words trying to hold back his tears finally answers, "I know them well, and they are conjoined twins." The doctors go back in the room with Pastor Butler to take another look at the men since they know they were conjoined twins. Butler sees them lying apart from each other for the first time and is horrified by the sight of one of them missing a side of his face which is dangling off the side of the other one; part of his face was peeled off which the doctors mistook as extra skin. Pastor Butler told the doctors the twins were joined at the head; then the doctors understood why they could not save them. Pastor Butler prayed a prayer thanking God for welcoming his good servants' home then left the room in tears; he cried all the way home not sure if he stopped at any of the traffic lights. He lost two good people that were near and dear to him; now he has to tell his wife and contact their family.

School finally started and would be Sasha's first time being in class all day without Shannon being nearby; Shannon is in middle school and little James had to be put in a special school. Sasha felt scared being without her older sister to protect her; most of the time she had to protect little James from the bullies which always gets her in trouble with the bigger kids and Shannon is needed for that. During the summer she became good friends with the Butler girls Tara and Lisa. Lisa is a year older so Sasha will be riding the bus to school with her; and Tara is in school at the church where her mom teaches pre-k. Sasha and Lisa ended up in the same class because Barbara would not allow them to put her in fourth grade; she felt she was too small and not mature enough. Sasha's test scores put her at high school level but her parents are too ignorant to understand that they have a little genius on their hand. Lisa introduced Sasha to more of her friends and showed her around the school so she wouldn't get lost in case she wasn't there. After having lunch Sasha was getting tired; there was a lot more reading and writing to do than what she was use to. She even fell asleep on the bus going home; and once she got in the house she went straight to bed. It took her a few weeks to adjust to the long hours of being in school all day. Shannon as usual made a lot of new friends with no fighting to fit in; but she had to deal with older boys liking her. Most of the girls her age were giggling with excitement at the thought of having older boys notice them; but Shannon found it to be irritating. She just wanted to enjoy being a little girl for a change and have fun doing it. She would always tell the boys she was too young and cannot have a boyfriend at this time. Little James was put in special classes to help him with his inability to read and write. They did not force him to stop using his left hand to write with they encouraged him to use it; and he never wanted to miss a day of school. Lisa was a big help to Sasha helping her adjust to being in class all day. Lisa made sure Sasha knew who the bad kids were around the neighborhood her age as she noticed Sasha was shorter than all of them. Lisa and Sasha's bus stop was in front of an empty apartment building that many of the children would run in and out of through the broken windows. Sasha and Lisa would not play in the building with the other kids so the other girls did not like them. One morning while they were sitting on the steps of the building talking as they were waiting for the bus; one of the bad girls decided she would fight Lisa for not letting the new girl play with them. She walked up to Lisa and slapped her on her head; but before Lisa could react Sasha had already jumped up and was beating the girl on the ground as she sat on top of her hitting her. Lisa managed to get Sasha off the girl as she noticed Sasha was out of control fighting the girl. The little girl got up and ran home just as the bus was pulling up flashing its lights for them to get on. It all happened so fast the other kids inside the building did not get a chance to see it. The two sat in their seat laughing about it all the way to school as Lisa described to Sasha what she looked like fighting out of control. "I forgot to cry after she hit me on my head, and it hurt too!" Lisa said laughing. Sasha replied, "It is official, you are my friend if I beat somebody up for hitting you." They looked each other eye to eye and burst out in laughter again; the day past without Sasha falling asleep on the bus ride home. The next morning as they walked to the bus stop they began talking about seeing angels as Lisa was so fascinated with Sasha's experience with seeing them. The other kids were grouped together mad about Sasha beating up their friend; so they waited for the two girls to get to the bus stop so they could beat them up. Something strange began to happen in the sky above them as Sasha and Lisa approached the other kids; it's like the moon got bigger, brighter and began to come down towards them. Sasha pointed up and said, "Look at the moon it's growing big and falling." Lisa looked up and said, "That's no moon, it's a blessing angel; God sends one down every year to grant a blessing." The object got brighter as it got closer to the children; but they all got scared screamed and ran into the building except Sasha. She stood still as the bright light came over her; she spoke out saying, "God please bless me with a normal family, that's all I want." It was silent for what seemed like forever to Sasha as she stood in the midst of a fog like substance. Its peaceful here as she's not worried about not getting an answer. Then a bright light flashed and it was over. The others came out of the building and asked her if she was okay, she smiled and shook her head to say yes. They were standing there quiet until the bus came and they all sat in their seats glad to get away from the spooky bus stop. Lisa asks Sasha, "What did you ask for?" Sasha smiled and said, "If I tell you it will not come to pass."

After months of working over-time James was finally able to come home at a decent hour only to find the apartment empty. Everybody was either at a friend's house or church; he was mad about it at first because dinner was not being cooked. He then remembered Barbara never cooked dinner for the kids. It's near the end of fall and construction work is starting to slow down; James is coming home early and going fishing with a guy he met at work. His friend had a boat which made it easier go out far in the gulf; James loved fishing out in the deep waters. One day he came home early after working only a half a day to find the kids home not in school. He quickly ask, "What ya'll doin home from school?" Shannon deliberately didn't answer him; but little James quickly said, "Teacher duty day no school." James gave Shannon a mean nasty look; he couldn't believe she wouldn't answer his question. Shannon on the other hand wouldn't look at her dad; she didn't care to answer him. She hated the fact that he was home with them; it means her name was going to be called more than she wanted it to be. Before her dad could say anything to her Barbara came out the room and smiled once she saw him and said, "You're home mighty early; is everything okay at work?" He answered, "Yeah, work slowing down is all. I'm going to take a bath; you wanna go out to lunch and hang out with me since I'm home early?" Barbara was surprised he asked her to go anywhere with him. She cheerfully said, "Yes." While he was in the bathroom the voices in her head kept repeating to her; he still wants the girl, you know he still wants the girl. She looks over at Shannon who is more interested in the book in her hand than what's going on around her. Barbara said to her, "Shan keep an eye on the children and don't ya'll leave this house." Shannon said, "Okay mom." They both left as Shannon got up went in the kitchen to fix something for lunch. After eating Shannon got the necklace with the house key and said to the others, "Come on let's go play." Little James protested saying, "No, mom said for us not to leave the house!" Shannon turns to look at him and says, "Really! When have they ever cared about us leaving the house? Name one," she demanded. With no answer in mind he put his head down and proceeded to walk out the door. They went down the street to play with the kids they met in vacation bible school during the summer. The children here were nice but nothing like Boynton where the parents treated you like family. Shannon was really missing her friends Wanda and Eddy Gal along with the gang in Boynton; there you were a part of a family, here it's every man for himself and that thought alone scared Shannon. She suspects her dad moved them here to get her away from her protection. After a few hours of play time they went home to have dinner and go to bed she hoped without their parents being home. She was glad no one was there yet; as predicted she knew they would not be back any time soon. She turned on the TV for Sasha and James then went in her room to be alone; she's been doing that a lot lately. She wishes Claire was here to talk to and pray the troubles away; but all she could do here was sit in the room and cry them away. Mrs. Butler was always too busy helping with church members; she barely had time to be with her own kids. There was a knock at the door just as she decided to come out and get the kids ready for bed. She yelled out, "Who is it?" It was one of the guys from the apartment down stairs. "It's Randy from down stairs, I noticed you kids are home alone; is everything okay?" Shannon hesitated to answer at first, she'd completely forgotten about the three men living down stairs. "We're fine Mr. Randy thank you for your concern." Randy didn't expect her to open the door to talk to him as he would have advised her not to; he yells back through the door, "Well I just wanted you kids to know if you need anything we are here for you. You don't have to be afraid to be here alone just to let you know; have a good night." She yells back, "Thank you Mr. Randy, good night." Shannon felt a little at ease knowing there was someone looking out for them as she made sure Sasha and James took a bath. Little James went in his room and fell asleep right away. Sasha shared a room with Shannon she would not have it no other way. An angel told her their daddy was a bad man and he wanted to hurt Shannon; so Sasha would not sleep in her own bed because she felt she needed to be close to Shannon to protect her. Shannon made sure the house was locked and went to bed thanking God for sending good people to look after them. She told Sasha about the three men down stairs looking out for them; so the two prayed for God to protect the good men down stairs. James and Barbara came home very late; he was drunk and she was a little tipsy. She managed to get him upstairs and in the bed as they both knocked out for the rest of the night. The kids were up early Saturday morning; Shannon cooked breakfast and they were sitting down eating and watching cartoons on the TV. By nine Shannon went in the kitchen to wash the dishes and frowns at doing it because it's another reason why she hates living in this place. She mumbles to herself, "When am I going to get a chance to be a child?" She starts to cry as she thinks about all she has been doing for them since she was four years old. She didn't know Sasha was standing next to her as she mumbled until she said, "I can help you clean so you can be a child again." Little James ran up to her and said, "I wanna help you be a child too, what can I do to help?" Shannon dried her tears and said to them, "We ate together; we may as well clean together." They promised to help her out as much as they can so she could be a kid too. They finished cleaning and went back to watching a little more cartoon then went out to play. Barb and James slept until late afternoon with James waking up with a hang-over. She got dressed after taking a bath and went to the kitchen to fix something to eat for the two of them. She found everything to be cleaned with no children in the house; she'd quickly fallen back in the mode of not caring where her children went as long as they were away from her. A small voice inside was telling her she should be concerned about him hurting Shannon again; but he had started back giving her all his attention and she was not giving that up for nothing. She ignored the small voice and continued to fix their food. She will do a lot of things to make James happy; but deep down inside she know she will never trust him around Shannon again; the voices in her head keeps telling her to watch him no matter what. James knows his wife loves the party life which is why he's going to make sure she gets it. He hopes it will keep her away from Shannon long enough for him to get her for what she'd done to him in Boynton. He plans to take Barb out every time he gets home early or have a day off. She's not much of a drinker, but she sure does love to dance the night away. He's going to make sure she is set in the party mood to where she wouldn't miss him if he slipped away. James is about to find out things don't always go as you plan it.

Doug had leased the apartment for six months; it's now getting close to Halloween and November was just a week away and nothing has happened yet. He was telling the guys to start packing everything but leave a couple cameras around the apartment and one inside James apartment. It was a warm Saturday morning they started packing when the guys saw Barbara get in the car with Susie off to go shopping she yells to the kids. James earlier that morning went to work a few hours of over-time; he gave

Barbara a big roll of cash to go shopping to keep her busy for a while. Doug and the guys had loaded some of the equipment in their van when they saw James come home early; Doug quickly ran in the house so James would not recognize him. Randy stopped James to introduce himself and find out what James was up to. They knew he was either coming in to go fishing with his friend or taking Barbara out to bars; but this time neither one of them seems to be around. The children are upstairs looking at cartoons after eating breakfast; they know this because they went up there to install a camera after a light bulb conveniently went out and no parent was home. Randy was being nice using small talk with James to get the information out of him, "I notice you sometimes go fishing with your buddy from work; when I'm not traveling long distance I love being out on the water fishing, it relaxes me. I was wondering if you and your friend won't mind me coming with you guys the next time you go out. I'm still trying to learn may around the city don't quite know where the good spots are yet. James was glad to know his neighbor was a fishing man. He wanted to talk fishing with him a little while longer but he was a man on a mission at the moment all he said, "Sure man, we'll be going out tomorrow morning early; I got something to do right now I'll get with you in a little bit later to tell you more." He shook Randy's hand and ran up stairs like a crazy man up to no good. Randy quickly ran to the others to let them know something was about to go down. Shannon and Sasha were in the kitchen cleaning while little James sat and watched cartoons. Their dad burst through the door looking mad as a bull pointed to Shannon in the kitchen and said, "Your ass is mine now, and nobody is here to save you." All three kids screamed and ran towards their rooms. Little James got to his room first closed his door and locked it leaving the girls to defend themselves. Sasha tripped over the big pot she still had from the kitchen; but just as she went down James jumped over her to get to Shannon. He grabbed her before she could get to her door and threw her in his room. She hit the side of the bed and managed to get to her feet and jumped to the other side like a jack rabbit before he could get to her. He tried to close and lock the door so she wouldn't escape but the door wouldn't close for some reason. He had no time to stop and figure out why that was happening; Shannon was fast on her feet and he had to find a way to get a hold of her. She was smart enough to keep the bed between them and stay away from his long arm reach; but she knew to stay away from the closet and the room was only so big. James was getting wildly angry and frustrated with the stupid door for coming open every time he'd lunge towards Shannon. She'd always escape his reach and make a run for the open door; but he was closer to it and would block her path to get out. She would somehow slip pass him being such a fast runner; and like a gazelle her long limbs propel her up over the bed to the other side. She see Sasha on the floor outside the door holding the big pot in place keeping the door from closing giving her a way out. Sasha is giving it her all keeping that pot in the door when Shannon screams to her, "Go get help, leave me! Go get help!" Sasha panics as she gets up and runs in the kitchen grabs a butcher knife then runs back to the door just as Shannon comes close to it but is blocked again. Sasha see that she is small enough to fit between the opening but before she could put her head through James blocks her view of her sister. Acting out of sheer desperation she sticks her hand in with the knife between his legs and tosses it as Shannon quickly darts by him; Sasha gets up and runs to the door for help. Shannon slips through his grip again but manage to catch the knife her sister threw in the room and once again she jumps to the other side of the bed and lands by the window with the knife hidden behind her against the wall. She thinks to herself; "I have to make one last attempt for the door to distract him, he doesn't know I have the knife." She fakes a move for the door and James does just what she expected him to do; she frantically snatches the cover off the bed and tosses it over towards the door. Just as James lunge towards the door to block the cover lands on him blinding him from seeing what she is doing. With all her might and a lot of help from her adrenalin, Shannon lifts the mattress off the bed and shoves it towards James knocking him off balance. James and the mattress fall to the floor with him on top of it. The mattress is partially on the box spring and has pinned the pot between the door and its frame; no one can get in or out without knocking the door off its frame. Barbara and Susie pull up outside laughing hilariously about their shopping spree. Barbara gets out of the car with both arms loaded with bags. Sasha comes running out of the house screaming, "He's trying to hurt her!" Barbara dropped all the bags and ran up stairs crying and screaming, "No, no, no!" Doug came out from hiding in the apartment ran and grabbed Sasha then handed her to Randy to calm her down then ran back up stairs. Barbara burst through the door knocking it down off the hinge onto the mattress beside James who is screaming for his life as Shannon is standing over him about to stab him with the knife. Like a mad crazy woman Barbara yells out, "Leave my child alone!" She jumps on him and starts biting and punching him not noticing that Shannon is about to stab him. Shannon jumps out of the way of her parents fight and runs out the door. She gets to the living room just as Doug is rushing in to what is happening; he grabs her and asks, "Are you okay? Where is he?" She points down the hall to the bed room. He runs down the hall to the room and finds a broken door next to James on top of Barbara choking her to death. He charges in and knocks him off Barbara just as she is about to pass out. The two men violently punch one another as if they are fighting for their lives. Barbara somehow manages to crawl out in the hallway where Shannon pulls her to the front door to get some fresh air; she is barely able to catch her breath and passes out. Shannon screams as Randy and Tony rushes up to her picks Barbara up and carries her down to the van to rush her to the hospital with Shannon in tow. Little James comes out his room thinking all was clear because there were no more screaming going on. He looks into his parents tore up room to see Doug hit his dad so hard and knocks him out; the big tall man he has been afraid of for years hit the floor fast and hard. It was the first time little James was able to look at his dad and not be afraid he was going to hurt him. He recognized the man that threw the punch; it was Mr. Stanley's driver. He walks over to Doug and asks, "Is he dead?" Doug answers, "No not yet; forgetting he was talking to a child. Doug looked down at the kid and said, "I didn't mean it like that son, he's going to be okay." The boy looked up at Doug and answered, "No need to feel bad about it, I sometimes wishes he were dead." Doug shook it off grabbed James by his legs and drags him to the door. Susie steps to the door just as Doug drops James legs down and walks out past her; she doesn't know what to say or think about what just happened in front of her. She takes little James by the hand and says, "Come on, I'm taking you and Sasha to the hospital to be with your mom and Shannon." As she was driving to the hospital her mind was trying to comprehend the events only to end up being more confused. There were too many questions popping up that she didn't have answers for. One thing is for sure; the stuff Barbara was telling about her life was not adding up to this. Susie wanted to know what was going on but was not sure if she should ask the kids. Some people train their kids not tell their in home business to others; and some kids you ask is like opening a floodgate of information you'd wish you hadn't ask. Susie decided not to bother asking the children they look like they've been through enough already; and judging by the drama taking place around her it's best if she not know. She decides some questions are best left unanswered and just be a help to them where it is needed. She sat with them for about an hour until Doug came and told her she can go home and get some rest. He told her he was their god parent and it was okay; she hesitated to leave them with this strange man who looked suspicious to her. Sasha and little James ran up to him and acknowledged him so she decided it was safe for her to leave them with him. Two hours later Doug was taking the children back to the apartment after the doctor told them Barbara would be okay she just has to stay in the hospital for a couple of days. Doug says to Shannon, "It's over, while she is gone get a suitcase for each of you and put all that you can fit in them; you will be leaving here when she comes back." Shannon shook her head in agreement and went in the rooms to pull out three large suitcases to begin packing. As she finished she took each suitcase to the living room and placed it by the front door. Finally she sat on the sofa and let out a sigh of relief as she remembers seeing Doug with Mr. Stanley driving his big car from time to time last year. Stanley told her before they left that he would not let her dad hurt her again. Tears began to well up in her eyes as she realized that Stanley sent Doug to protect her. She didn't ask what happened to her dad because she didn't care to know; she was glad to be finally getting away from him for good. Little James kept it to himself what he saw Doug do to his dad. He was playing his imaginary game rolling on the floor as if he didn't have a care in the world; and he didn't because he no longer had a reason to be afraid. Sasha was sitting quiet in a chair trying to wrap her child mind around why she had to decide to help kill her dad to save her sister. She was getting angry at the whole situation and did not quite understand why it had to turn out the way it did. All she ever wanted was to be in a normal loving family and is angered to find out her family is not normal; something is broken and she doesn't know how to find what it is. Shannon hasn't noticed the change in Sasha's behavior; usually she is very attentive what is going on with Sasha, now she is too busy imagining life without being attacked.

Doug goes over to Pastor Butler to explain and settle the damage done to the apartment. Stanley has him to pay the Pastor far above what the damage is worth. At first Pastor Butler would not take the money because he wanted to know about the well being of the family. But because Doug kept putting a stack of cash in front of him rather than answer any questions concerning the family he took the money. After Doug left Pastor really begins to worry about the people he rented the place to; he began to question why God had him to rent to that family. He headed out in the prayer garden to pray about it when he saw Sasha sitting on his prayer bench crying. "What has you in the prayer garden crying Sasha?" He asked, being cautious with his approach. Sasha looks out him as he sits down besides her and answers, "Pastor, we are moving and I don't understand why God couldn't just give me a normal family; I just want us to be normal." Pastor Butler is over come with emotions as he picks up Sasha and holds her in his lap and prays to God as she cries. When he is done praying Sasha is sleep; he takes his handkerchief and wipes her face then carries her home to lay her down. Pastor Butler is feeling nervous about why this little girl is so torn about having a normal family. He'd already noticed the parents weren't spending time with the kids; but at the same token the girls are great workers in the church and the community, and are highly spiritually gifted. Shannon lets him in to lay Sasha down in her bed and then they sit down in the living room and talk. Shannon tells him everything that has been happening in their family mainly with her. Pastor Butler's heart is heavy and broken listening to Shannon's story; he's so over come with emotions he just grabs Shannon's hands and began to pray and cry to the lord for his mercy to be upon her. As he was leaving she assured him she would be fine now that they are moving away from him. Pastor saw that things were packed and boxed up he was relieved to see that; but he worried about them still being alone with a mother whose mental state is unstable. He went home and decided to add the family on the church prayer list.

Doug went to the hospital to pick up Barbara as Tony and Randy took James to a boat they had on the docks and left him there bound until they return to deal with him later. Barbara came home and began packing up her suitcase as a moving truck is backed in alongside the stairs outside the apartments. A limo was waiting in the alley for Barb and her kids to take them back to her parents' home town Deleon Springs. The movers will pack both places during the night as Doug reserved a storage unit in the city of Deland for two years or until she find a place; it's not far from her parents' town. They left in the limo with their suitcases hoping for a better life ahead; that is what Shannon is hoping for. It was a quiet long ride down the highway as Barb still was not able to talk; but she had a pad and pen in hand to write whatever she needed to say. Nobody asked Doug what happened to James; considering what all he took them through no one wanted to know.

Meanwhile back on the boat; James woke up to him about to be thrown overboard off a boat. He grabbed the man that was trying to toss him over and both men went into the water. James found himself once again having to fight for his life as both men struggle in the water. Tony foolishly untied James after Doug warned him not to untie him because he is very strong and a damn good fighter. After Doug left Tony did what he was told not to do; Tony feels he is young and strong enough to handle any man who comes his way. Tony is regretting that choice as he finds himself fighting for his life deep in the Gulf of Mexico as the empty boat rocks from side to side above them. The man pops up from being deep beneath the water grasping for air as he grabs the ladder hanging on the side of the boat. He's tired and his heart is beating hard and fast as realizes he just survived the fight of his life; He starts the engine and heads to shore. He docks the boat then ties it off before walking away he looks out to see if there was any sign of the other body floating, nothing. As he walks away James thinks to himself that's the second time he almost died fooling with that girl. "Never again" he says out loud and continues walking down the road being thankful he is alive. Finally he makes it back to the apartment seeing all of his belongings on a pile in the alley. He packs what he could in a suitcase that was there and heads to a hotel. He can't believe he just threw away all that was important to him because he was just too stupid to leave well enough alone. Speaking out loud he says, "Now I'm alone, lesson learned James; lesson learned."

Made in the USA
Columbia, SC
07 April 2023